THE
HOUSE
ON THE
LAKE

A Selection of Recent Titles by Julie Ellis from Severn House

AVENGED
BEST FRIENDS
DEADLY OBSESSION
GENEVA RENDEZVOUS
THE HOUSE ON THE LAKE
THE ITALIAN AFFAIR
NINE DAYS TO KILL
NO GREATER LOVE
SECOND TIME AROUND
SINGLE MOTHER
VANISHED
VILLA FONTAINE
WHEN THE SUMMER PEOPLE HAVE GONE

THE
HOUSE
ON THE
LAKE

.

Julie Ellis

2237 9818

This title first published in Great Britain 2000 by
SEVERN HOUSE PUBLISHERS LTD of
9–15 High Street, Sutton, Surrey SM1 1DF.
This title first published in the USA 2000 by
SEVERN HOUSE PUBLISHERS INC of
595 Madison Avenue, New York, N.Y. 10022.

British Library Cataloguing in Publication Data

Ellis, Julie, 1933-
   The house on the lake
   1.   Romantic suspense novels
   I.   Title
   813.5'4 [F]

   ISBN 0-7278-5521-2

All situations in this publication are fictitious and
any resemblance to living persons is purely coincidental.

Printed and bound in Great Britain by
MPG Books Ltd, Bodmin, Cornwall.

FOR BETTY LYNNE AND HOWIE.

Chapter One

With no inkling that my life was about to undergo a shattering upheaval, I enjoyed a quiet taxi ride down Lexington Avenue through the light Saturday afternoon traffic to the side entrance to Grand Central Station. I thought I was en route to nothing more momentous than a convivial cocktail party in suburbia.

Once inside Grand Central I hurried to the information booth to learn the gate number of my train. It was ready to take passengers and I went aboard.

The two other United Nations secretaries with whom I shared an apartment in the East Seventies had planned a party for this evening, but Eric Svedborg, whose secretary I had been for almost a year, had insisted I attend his cocktail party. He had recently returned from six weeks in Europe and Asia on UN business, and while he was gone his wife had successfully transferred the family into their newly purchased Connecticut estate.

"There will be some interesting young people," he'd coaxed me. "You'll enjoy the party."

I saw the glint in his eyes. He was an incurable romantic. I knew there must be some young man that he was determined that I meet.

I was glad that I'd boarded the train early. On weekends in late June great numbers of New Yorkers were suburbia-bound for the day. I staked out a seat by a window and settled down to read my paperback.

After the first page I found it difficult to concentrate. My mind kept wandering to the fifteen-day tour of Scandinavia I planned to take with Kathy and Betty Lynne, my two roommates. I'd never been to Europe despite my obsession with foreign languages, which had brought me my UN job. I dreamt wistfully of winters skiing in the Alps, spring vacations in Paris, autumn in Rome. Hardly likely on a UN secretary's salary!

In front of me a corpulent, eighty-year-old woman in a mink stole was avidly discussing her last summer's European travels with the man beside her.

"Oh, I tell you, you haven't lived until you've seen Europe. Of course, they hate us over there," she conceded conscientiously, "and the thievery is unbelievable. But when you come home you remember the good parts, and it's marvelous."

I sat back, the paperback open in my lap, and wove fantasies about my "glorious fifteen days in magnificent Scandinavia," never guessing, then, the strange, dramatic switch in my destination.

The train pulled into my sun-drenched station. Taxis were waiting, as I'd been promised. I piled into a group taxi, discovering that one other fare was also bound for the Svedborg party. He was a Belgian attached to the UN and bore a remarkable resemblance to my mother's current husband.

Of course, I couldn't remember my own father—he died when I was barely two, but Mother had a talent for marrying delightful men. I had been painfully upset, along with my two half-sisters, when Mother divorced her second husband eight years ago. I was glad that I was going away to college when she married her present husband, though, again, she married a charming man.

I was guilt-ridden because I felt such deep sympathy for my stepfathers. Mother, spoiled and capricious, had once been a great beauty. She made incessant demands on her husbands. After college I'd headed immediately for New York, determined to be independent and not to be a party to this new marriage.

The Svedborg house was about four miles from the railroad station, set high on a hill. It was an elegant colonial set above a series of picturesque terraces formed by fieldstone embankments. Abundant mountain laurel and rose bushes bloomed on the three acres that surrounded the house.

8

Teckla Svedborg, tall and attractive, hovered at the door greeting new arrivals. The living room was huge and furnished with beautiful antiques. It was already crowded with guests, as was, to a lesser extent, the adjoining den.

"We must talk about your trip," Mrs. Svedborg said enthusiastically, warmly taking my hand. "I will give you the names of some people to look up in Stockholm. They are so fond of Americans. They will show you around."

Mrs. Svedborg introduced me to a towering young man, entranced with his first look at America. I discovered he came from Malmo, Sweden. For a little while we talked about the Swedish couple from Malmo who were writing popular mysteries.

But I noticed he was intrigued by a tall, sun-bronzed blonde across the room. Only my extreme slimness gives me the appearances of being tall. I came barely to his shoulders. My hair is near black, my eyes blue, my skin milk white despite yearly efforts to acquire a golden tan. Philosophically I released him and joined a trio of UN people, whom I knew by sight.

"You American secretaries are the most beautiful in the world," a portly Italian with an infectious grin told me with admiration. Then he squinted in concentration, his eyes skimming past me to someone being greeted at the door. "Did you say your name was Laval?"

"Yes, Andrea Laval," I repeated, accepting a cocktail from a tray being circulated by the Svedborgs' teenage son.

"Wait," he said with amusement. "You must meet another Laval. A Frenchman who now lives in Geneva. Years ago he was with us at the UN. Excuse me, please—but stay here," he exhorted.

He left us, manipulating with astonishing agility through the thronged living room. I watched with amusement as he corralled the new arrival, prodded him towards the fireplace where I stood with a woman translator and a South African delegate who spoke with fervor about his country's future. En route the new guest acquired a cocktail and exchanged pleasantries with several guests.

He was in his late forties, trim, still quietly handsome. His dark hair was marked with distinguished touches of grey. His eyes were brown and serious. A charming man, I decided, even before we spoke.

9

"This is Armand Laval," the Italian said with relish. "Armand, you must meet another Laval. Perhaps you two will discover some common cousins."

"I'm Andrea Laval," I said, and paused because he was suddenly ashen.

"Andrea?" He repeated. His eyes searching my face. "Andrea Laval?"

"Yes." I was unnerved by the intensity of his scrutiny. Why was he staring at me this way?

"Will you excuse us, please?" he said brusquely to the others, and then firmly guided me away from them towards the less-crowded den. I was bewildered.

In the far corner of the large den, Armand Laval gently urged me into one of a pair of small chairs that flanked the ceiling-high bookcases. The hand which held his martini shook so badly his drink threatened to spill. *What was happening?* What did my name mean to him?

"Andrea," he asked unsteadily, "what was your mother's name? Tell me, please."

"Marcy," I said. "Marcy Weston before her first marriage. Are we—are we related?" I asked.

"Your father, Andrea," he asked urgently. "What did your mother tell you of him?"

"He died before I was two," I explained. "I don't remember him."

"No." Such anguish in his eyes. "That was a lie. He did not die." His voice acquired fresh strength. "Andrea, I am your father."

I stared at him. The words sank in, yet meant nothing. And then suddenly I felt encased in ice.

"My father is dead," I repeated.

"Andrea, I married Marcy Weston when I was with the French delegation to the UN. Twenty-three years ago. When you were almost two, I was transferred to Paris. I went ahead to rent a house for us, to prepare for your mother and you. But she dropped completely out of sight. I was frantic, helpless. I hired detectives. They could find no trace of my family. There was no one on your mother's side to contact. Only cousins. They knew nothing." His eyes were grief-stricken in recall.

"But she has always told me my father was dead," I

10

stammered. My voice low, as his was, so that the others could not hear.

"That was her way!" he said with a rush of anger. "To become tired of people all at once. To dispose of what annoyed her. She had the audacity to steal all these years from us!"

I gazed earnestly at him. I could feel the sincerity in him reaching out to me.

"I don't know what to believe." My instinct was to believe him. But what about my mother? Could she have lied about something as important in my life as this? To deny me my father all these years?

"Andera, where does your mother live now?" he asked with an effort to be calm.

"In a suburb of Chicago. She's married again. Twice since—" My voice ebbed away. How did I know she had ever been married to Armand Laval? Was this some grotesque error? Or was he my father?

"I received a letter from an attorney, informing me of the divorce. I assumed, of course, that she would remarry." His smile was sardonic. "She is, no doubt, still beautiful."

"Yes," I said softly. But so fearful of growing old. Always at the mirror, studying her face. Terrified of each new line.

"I flew to New York to question the attorney who handled the divorce," he continued. "I wanted my child. I demanded an address. Of course, she had disappeared again. Andrea," he reached for my hand, "I thought I would never see you again. And then I walk into a party, and Carlo Corelli is introducing me to my daughter!"

My mind was in a turmoil. *Was* he my father? How did I find out? One way.

"Would you—would you talk to my mother on the phone?" I asked, my voice unsteady. Always my mother avoided the unpleasant, so that even the children—my sisters and I—made a point of handling her as though she were a fragile porcelain statuette. But today she would have to face reality without velvet cushions.

He smiled at me with compassion that brought tears to my eyes. He knew the depths of my uncertainty. How desperately I needed some concrete proof of his identity. He rose to his feet, pulled me to mine.

"We will ask Teckla Svedborg if we may use a phone in one of the upstairs rooms," he said quietly. "Come."

In the exquisitely furnished master bedroom on the second floor of the Svedborg house I reached for the telephone and dialed my mother in a suburb of Chicago. I prayed she would be home. The man who said he was my father stood by a window, gazing sternly out onto the landscaped terrace below, where sunlight had now given way to grayness. A summer storm was threatening.

"Hello." My mother's provocative voice answered.

"Mother, it's Andrea," I said, gearing myself for the confrontation. Perhaps it was wrong, I thought with guilt, but I must do it this way. "I have someone here who wants to talk with you."

"Darling, whoever is it?" she began, but I was already handing the phone to Armand Laval.

"Marcy," he said drily, "this is Armand." He frowned in annoyance at something she said. "Armand Laval, Marcy. Surely you can remember your first husband!"

I stood beside him, watching him struggle to retain his composure. Knowing the anger, the hurt, the frustration of the years which churned within him. There was a singing in my head. No doubts now. This was my father.

He talked briefly, then handed the phone to me again. His face was taut as he walked to the window, gazed out again while I talked with my mother.

"Andrea, I had to do it this way." Mother's voice was faintly shrill. *How* could she have done this to my father and me? "He would have taken you away from me. I couldn't move with him to Europe—I'd die in all that strangeness. I had to keep you with me. My baby," she said dramatically. "I took what money we had and I opened a dress shop in that little town in Illinois. You were always happy, Andrea," she insisted with an air of vindication. "You didn't need him."

At last I put down the phone. Stood there trembling. I turned my eyes to my father, who had tried so desperately to find his family. Feeling the pain that must have plagued him. Knowing he had a daughter; not knowing where.

"Andrea." His voice broke. He reached for me. "My daughter."

12

* * *

We made no excuses for our sudden departure. But I sensed in Teckla Svedborg a comprehension that this was a poignantly special time for my father and me. Later she would be told. She would understand.

"I saw a small, interesting restaurant as I drove through town," my father recalled with quiet pleasure. "We will go there and have an early dinner together. So much I have to learn about you, Andrea," he said with beautiful tenderness. "All the years to span."

In a now heavy rain we drove through the winding hills down to Main Street, to park before a meticulously maintained eighteenth-century white colonial house that was now a restaurant. Hand in hand we darted from the car, across the sidewalk to the protection of the porch, entered the long narrow corridor to the main dining room at the rear.

In an aura of unreality I sat at a small, linen-covered table, listening to my father talk about the early days of his marriage, about his delight when I was born.

Our waiter came over. For a few minutes we were involved with the business of ordering. Melon, a paté, onion soup; duck à l'orange. We decided with delight that our tastes were similar.

"Andrea, I cannot believe this is happening." My father's hand reached over to cover mine. "The Svedborgs invite me to a party, and for old time's sake, I go—and find such richness." His smile was incandescent. "So much I wish to know. Where do we begin? You have yet to meet your grandmother. Your half sister Lisette." His smile faded. His eyes grew somber. "There was a brother. Lisette's twin. Six years ago, when they were six, Michel and his mother died in a tragic boating accident. My mother—your grandmother—has lived with me ever since, helping to raise Lisette."

"I can't believe it." I shook my head slowly. "A grandmother. A sister. And a father." Tenderness surged in me. "Even when I was little, Mother told me my sisters' father was my stepfather. He was a good father to me, the years Mother remained married to him," I acknowledged, "but I was always wistful about not having a father of my own. I

13

would make up stories—you know the way a child does this. Pretending."

"We will make up for those empty years, Andrea," he promised. "You must come to Switzerland and stay with us. For a while, at least. I come regularly to the United States on business. Never again will we lose touch, Andrea. Wait," he said suddenly, "why don't you come to us for the summer? We are in the vacation house on the side of the mountain forty kilometers from Geneva. It is beautiful there. You will come," he said firmly.

"I have three weeks vacation in August," I said slowly. My heart pounded. "I'd planned on spending fifteen days in Scandinavia. I can cancel the reservations."

"Come for a month," he coaxed, a lilt in his voice. "Your employer will allow you this. Come to the Chateau Laval," he said humorously, "and meet your grandmother and your sister."

"Yes," I promised with a surge of anticipation. "I'll come for the month of August," not knowing then what that month would bring to me.

Chapter Two

As I emerged from the elevator in the carpeted corridor that led to our seventeenth-floor, so-called luxury apartment, I could hear festive sounds that indicated our party was in full swing. Someone was singing folk rock to the accompaniment of a guitar.

I wished wistfully that the party was over and that I could sit down with Kathy and Betty Lynne and tell them what had happened at the Svedborgs'. I had a compulsion to share this sudden upheaval in my life. Still, I walked in an air of unreality, though these few hours with my father had been very real. Poignantly sweet. Hours I would treasure for the rest of my life.

I found my key, unlocked the door, walked inside. Over the din Kathy called to me to tell me my mother had telephoned.

"You're to call her back collect," Kathy reported.

Smiling at the cluster of guests, most of whom I knew, I strode into the bedroom I shared with Kathy. I didn't want to call my mother but I knew I must.

I sat at the edge of the bed, reached for the phone, dialed. What could my mother say that would make any difference now?

"Andrea, why did it take you so long to call me back?" Mother demanded aggrievedly.

"I was in Connecticut," I explained, struggling to remain cool. "I just walked into the apartment."

"What an awful thing for Armand to put you through!"

15

How easily she could reverse a situation! "He could have handled the situation less dramatically."

"It doesn't matter, Mother." What mattered was that she had lied to me all these years.

"Andrea, I never allowed you to suffer," she reminded me virtuously. "I opened up that dress shop and I supported both of us." For seven months, I thought. Seven months after my father's supposed death she'd married my stepfather, obviously having acquired a divorce in the interim. She never worked again, but how many times I heard about the months she slaved in the dress shop to support her baby. "The marriage to Armand was a mistake in the beginning. I was a child." I refrained from reminding her she'd been over twenty-one. "His mother warned him it was a mistake. She said it would never work. How could he expect me to desert my own country to live in Europe?"

"I'm going over to spend the month of August with him," I tried to sound matter-of-fact. "In his house near Geneva."

"What about the Scandinavian trip?" she demanded. She was furious with me. "Are you giving that up?"

"Mother, I think this is more important," I said gently. She paused.

"I didn't ask Armand. Did he ever remarry?"

"His wife died in an accident six years ago. I have a half sister who's twelve." I heard myself saying these things as though in a dream. "His mother is raising her." My grandmother. Grandmère, Lisette would call her. A whole new family. Frightening and intriguing, simultaneously.

"Andrea, I don't want you to go over to visit him." Mother's voice was edged with hysteria. "His mother hated me, even though we never met. If you go there, something awful will happen. I feel it, Andrea."

"Mother, I'm going," I said quietly. "I have to do this."

*   *   *

I was relieved when the last of the guests were gone. Kathy and Betty Lynne wore the glow that told of another successful party. With the first pink streaks of dawn lighting the sky, we all sank down on the sofa for a final cup of coffee. I told Betty Lynne and Kathy, haltingly, conscious

16

of their shock, about the encounter with my father.

"Wow!" Kathy leaned forward avidly. "Like something out of a forties movie!"

"Andrea, do you honestly think you ought to run off to Switzerland that way?" Betty Lynne stared somberly at me. "I mean, without any investigation? What do you know about him?"

"Betty Lynne, he's my father." I was shocked at such reserve.

"What did your mother say?" Betty Lynne probed.

"She—she was astonished." I hesitated. I couldn't tell them that it would be a long time before I could think about my mother without anger. I couldn't tell them she was willful, capricious, self-centered. "She doesn't want me to visit him," I added, and was immediately angry with myself for this admission. They couldn't know how illogical Mother was.

"I don't think you should go," Betty Lynne said, reinforcing Mother.

"Why?" Color warmed my face. Nothing could stop me from flying to Geneva. Suddenly the trip was the most important thing in my life. "Just because we've been separated all these years?"

"I don't know." She squinted in thought, then shrugged. "Call it bad vibrations."

"Oh, come off it," Kathy scoffed. "I think it's marvelous. Of course Andrea should go. It's like a jet age fairy tale. Grace Kelly married the Prince and Andrea Laval finds her father."

"First thing Monday I'm canceling the Scandinavian reservations—" I stopped dead. "It's not as though you can't have fun without me," I said guiltily.

"We'll do great," Kathy said firmly.

"I hope I can get a seat on such short notice," I said anxiously. "It's the height of the season."

"The 747s never fly loaded," Kathy reminded me. "You'll get a seat." She stifled a yawn. "Let's go to bed. I'm dead."

We slept into the early afternoon, lounged around the apartment the rest of the day, swapping sections of the Sunday *Times*. In my mind I kept improvising speeches to Mr. Svedborg, explaining why it was urgent I have a whole month's vacation rather than the arranged three weeks. I had developed a compulsion to spend a whole month in Switzerland. I wanted to have time to get to know my grandmother and Lisette. To know my father.

Monday morning I awoke with a start, to the shrill ring of the alarm. I was still caught in the unreality that had swept me up at the Svedborg party, realizing subconsciously that today I must explain our precipitate departure.

I tossed aside the covers and fumbled for my slippers. Yawning, I headed for the kitchenette to put on the morning coffee.

I was meeting my father for lunch. What a lovely phrase —"my father". We were meeting at my favorite little Greek restaurant at the corner of 49th Street and First Avenue. He was taking the 6:10 P.M. flight to Geneva. Already I felt a sense of loss.

Explanations to Mr. Svedborg were less difficult than I expected. He was warmly sympathetic and willing for me to take the extra time. Three hours later I hurried up First Avenue to the restaurant for lunch, with a sense of having entered a whole new world.

"I'm expecting someone," I told, the maître d' breathlessly.

"He's here." He smiled and nodded towards a table near the front.

I made my way through the narrow path between the tables to where my father waited for me with a welcoming smile.

"I have ordered wine for us. What would you like for lunch?"

Too quickly the hour was past. Dad walked with me along First Avenue in the June sunlight. We stood admiring the impressive lines of the UN complex, the stirring array of international flags on display outdoors. He chuckled at the busloads of school children converging on the UN—a daily sight to me but one Dad found amusing.

Dad saw me inside before he hailed a cab to take him back to the hotel. In a matter of hours he would be once more in Geneva.

Later in the afternoon I phoned the travel agent who had arranged our Scandinavian tour, asked him instead for a round-trip reservation to Geneva. In five weeks and three days I would be aboard a Swissair 747, bound for Geneva.

* * *

Kathy and Betty Lynne, on the first day of their own vacations, accompanied me to JFK. Betty Lynne, normally gregarious, was somber and quiet.

"What's the matter with you?" I chided with good humor while I waited to have my luggage weighed in. "You're two days away from flying off to Stockholm and you act as though the world is about to collapse."

"I wish you were going with us instead of to Geneva," she said doggedly. "I keep getting these bad vibrations."

"Honey, you get bad vibrations when somebody's going to spill a drink on my dress," Kathy reproached. "Don't frighten her."

We had a snack in the coffee shop, and then it was time for me to board the plane. I hadn't realized the massive dimensions of a 747 until now, the number of passengers it could accommodate. The woman ahead of me was almost in a panic when we were divided by sex for the preboarding search.

"Do you suppose we're going to be hijacked?" she asked anxiously.

"The search is routine," I soothed. "To make sure there's no chance of hijacking."

Ahead of us a pair of dungareed teenagers were philosophically parting with their boy scout knives. In the next line the men were being physically frisked. The women were delicately handled, with a woman airport employee gliding over each passenger with a metal detector.

"It's so terrible," the nervous passenger ahead of me said. "We're going on a pleasure trip."

"In a little over seven and a half hours we'll be landing at Geneva Airport," I said ebulliently. "Don't worry about our being hijacked. The odds are against it."

Inside the huge 747 I settled myself in my assigned seat with a sense of towering anticipation. Knowing I would face moments of painful strangeness, but never suspecting the terror, the dangers that lay ahead.

I ate my dinner without tasting it as I was caught up in

19

the beauty that lay outside the plane. I fantasized about the month that lay ahead of me. I tried to visualize my grandmother. Lisette. My grandmother was English by birth, multi-lingual as was Lisette, who was born in France. And here I come, I thought humorously. As American as hot dogs.

The trays were removed. Light blankets were distributed. I tried to sleep and, managed to dose for brief intervals. We'd be arriving in Geneva at 6:30 A.M. Swiss time. Back in New York it would be 1:30 A.M.

The night gave way to dawn and a magnificent sunrise as we moved closer to Switzerland. A cry of delight escaped me as we passed over the stark, gray Alps. Just ahead, a teenager with a movie camera was ecstatically shooting film.

Coming in towards the airport someone behind me was pointing out the Jet d'Eau, the famous Geneva fountain that spurts over four hundred feet into the air.

I was astonished at the speed with which we went through customs. In a matter of minutes, it seemed, I was in the strikingly modern area of the car rental booths, where I was to be met. My two oversized suitcases were in the hands of a porter.

"Andrea!" My father hurried towards me and pulled me close. "You are truly here!"

With his arm about me, he prodded me towards the doors that led to the parking lot at our right, instructing the porter in French.

"I told him the car is right outside," he translated for me, and then we both laughed because for the moment he had forgotten that I spoke fluent French. Though how my college French would stand up beside those who spoke it as a first language, I was unsure.

The car was a dark blue Bentley. The chauffeur—a small, dark, moustached man in his fifties—emerged quickly from behind the wheel to open the trunk for the porter. I tried to mask my astonishment. Not until this moment, seeing the chauffeured Bentley, had I realized my father was wealthy. He had described the house as the Chateau Laval, with a touch of humor. I'd thought it was a sort of family jest.

"Henri, take care of the porter," Dad said briskly, guiding me into the rear of the car. But not before I'd intercepted a look of such hatred on Henri's face that I recoiled. *Hatred for me.*

I sat back in the car. Shaken. Trying to tell myself I had imagined that vicious glare. Trying to display interest in my surroundings.

"You must be exhausted," Dad said with solicitude. "But you will be able to sleep all day, to catch up with the change in time."

"I'm too excited to be tired," I protested.

We drove from the parking lot, circled around in the direction of the auto-route. My eyes eagerly scanned the road signs. Paris! Several hours drive in the other direction I realized; but nonetheless, the road sign was an exotic sight to me.

"Ferney!" I exclaimed before Henri made the left onto the auto-route, craning my head for a clear view of the sign. "Is it near?"

"Only four miles from Geneva," Dad said with amusement. "We're quite near the French border, you know. One day we will drive to Ferney."

I settled back with a sigh of pleasure. To visit Ferney, where Voltaire spent the last years of his life! I forgot the unnerving hatred I'd seen on Henri's face. Oh, this month at the Chateau Laval would be a fantastic experience! Never guessing what lay ahead of me.

Traffic was light driving towards Lausanne, on this early Monday morning on the last day of July; but everything interested me. I was in Switzerland. A recurrent miracle to me.

To our right lay Lake Geneva. Postcard beautiful. Even this early in the morning a pair of sailboats skimmed the water. Beyond, was the magnificence of the mountains rising high into the clouds. The Alps I had seen as gray crags from above.

"What a marvelous blue," I said enthusiastically, my eyes sweeping the beauty of the lake.

"But even Lake Geneva has been touched by pollution," Dad told me, his voice deepening with sadness. "Sections of the lake are banned for swimming. Still," he added with a determined surge of optimism, "it is perhaps the most beautiful lake in the world. And the mountain there—" He

21

leaned forward intently, and my gaze followed his. How sharply etched the mountains were against the blueness of the sky! "The one rising tallest in the middle—that is Mont Blanc. Not on view every day," he conceded, "but on fair days such as this it is one of our great sights."

I gazed at a road sign just ahead.

"A hundred twenty kilometers an hour?" I asked in disbelief. "We're allowed such speed?"

Dad chuckled.

"Andrea, a kilometer is only five-eights of a mile," he explained. "Though some motorists prefer to consider it the equivalent of a mile," he admitted as a car zoomed past us. "We will turn off at Rolle," he said when Henri changed lanes, preparing for an exit. "Then we start climbing up the side of the mountain to the chateau. It is midway between Bougy Villars and Aubonne." He chuckled. "One is a village, the other a very small town," he explained in response to my look of inquiry. "You could not possibly have heard of either."

We left the auto-route, circled under a viaduct, past small, flourishing farmland. Now we were traveling on a narrow, country road that curved picturesquely around the side of the mountain, rising ever higher. We were in vineyard country. On both sides of the road, as far as the eye could see, grapevines grew tall and lush, heavy with clusters of not-yet-ripe grapes.

Soon we were driving through the village of Bougy Villars. Small, pastel, concrete houses with colorful shutters and flower-filled window boxes, lined each side of the narrow street. A dog ambled along, refusing to give way despite Henri's angry honk.

We passed a small country store not yet open for business, though the post office—despite the hour—invited customers with its open door. In a tiny garden where bees buzzed about a hive, a woman drinking coffee glanced up to smile at us. Dad nodded courteously. A pair of small children gazed at the car with interest. The village was just coming to life for another summer day that would be, I suspected, astonishingly hot.

We left the village behind. The houses were now less close together. The sun-bronzed men were already moving about the vineyards with hats to protect them. Below us was a tractor with a driver inventively using a beach umbrella to provide shade.

We moved higher up the side of the mountain so that we were gazing down now upon tier after tier of vineyards. The auto-route had become a narrow ribbon that lay along the lakeshore far below. A train chugged parallel to the auto-route, en route to Geneva.

I stifled a yawn and felt tiredness creeping up on me. I'd slept little on the plane. Back home it was barely two in the morning.

"You are tired," Dad said solicitously. "We will have breakfast together at the house, and then you must sleep. The house is just ahead."

Henri made a sharp left up a steep incline. Near the crest of the mountain, in a lushly wooded area, surrounded by a wide expanse of neatly trimmed lawn sat an impressively large, tall, immaculately white concrete chateau. Its many shutters were painted an audacious yellow, and wrought-iron balconies fronted several upper story windows. Balustraded terraces sprawled off the right and left wings of the structure and a front terrace led into a wide, low stairs at the entrance.

Rose bushes bloomed and red and pink geraniums were in extravagant display everywhere. Flowering shrubs banked the foundation of the house and outlined the lawns. To the left I spied a large swimming pool. Oh yes, I thought with optimism, this was going to be a glorious vacation.

The Bentley pulled up before the chateau.

"Home, Andrea," Dad said gently. "We have been here almost six years."

The anguish in his voice reminded me that six years ago his second wife and Lisette's twin—my half brother—died in the tragic boating accident. Plainly, he could not bear remaining in their house near Paris. He had moved with Lisette and her grandmother—my grandmother—to this house, to try to live with his grief.

"It's a lovely house," I said softly.

Henri opened the car door for us. We walked out into the crisp early morning air, fragrant with the scent of roses. Henri went to the trunk of the Bentley to bring out my suitcases.

23

As we walked up the stairs, the front door was opened by a small, rotund woman with graying hair and nearsighted eyes. She squinted at us as we approached.

"Claudine, I would like to introduce my daughter, Andrea," Dad said with a flourish.

"Bonjour, Mademoiselle," Claudine said stiffly. There was disapproval in her dark eyes, in the set of her thin lips.

"Bonjour, Claudine." I made my voice determinedly light. I would *not* show that I was disconcerted by this second display of disapproval.

"Claudine understands English well, but she is uneasy in speaking the language. It is all right, Claudine," Dad reassured her as he ushered me into the foyer. "Andrea speaks French."

The foyer walls and ceiling were austere white plaster, a dramatic background for the colorful modern paintings, the magenta carpeting, the massive black wrought-iron chandelier.

"Oh, what a handsome child!" I said involuntarily, pausing before a small painting that hung above a table in the hall along which Dad was guiding me. And then I was silent, my heart pounding. Because Claudine was staring at me with fierce intensity. With the same hatred I had seen in Henri. *Why did they feel this way toward me?*

"That is Michel," Dad said quietly, and turned to inspect my face. "He was very like you. The same delicate features, the same high cheekbones." Then, with an effort, he spoke to Claudine. "Claudine, please serve us breakfast in the family dining room."

Henri was going up the wide magenta-carpeted stairs with my suitcases. The car still remained out front. An early morning stillness was everywhere as Dad and I moved into the room to the left of the hall.

The family dining room was delightfully cheerful, with the sun shining in through an enormous picture window that looked out on the pool. Comfortable captain's chairs upholstered in the same striking blue-and-green print as the draperies at the picture window flanked the round oak table. Again, white plaster walls served as a background for two modern paintings and for the heavy oak shelves that were lined with a collection of exquisite, blown glass figures.

24

"I usually swim for about fifteen minutes each morning before I settle down to work," Dad explained while we seated ourselves at the table, "except for the two days a week that I go into Geneva while we are in residence here." He glanced at his watch with a wry smile. "Everyone is still asleep."

"I'm sorry to have dragged you out of bed so early," I apologized.

"I would have been there at any hour," he said. "You do not know what it means to me to have you here, after all these years. Later," he continued, forcing a casualness his eyes belied, "you will meet your grandmother and Lisette. And my secretary, Pat Fraser—" He smiled at my look of surprise. "Pat's Scotch-Irish, she has been with me eighteen years. She stays here with us for the summer months. Also, there is a young girl—Jeanne—who comes in for the day. And there you have our entire household."

Claudine came in, stern and taciturn, and set large white and black porcelain cups of steaming hot coffee before us. Perhaps she was annoyed at having to arise so early this morning, I decided guiltily.

I listened attentively while Dad told me with pride about Lisette's skill at the piano, her flair for languages, her fragile loveliness.

"Your grandmother is, perhaps, too demanding," he confided unhappily. "This summer she is insisting that Lisette be coached in English grammer in preparation for the fall. Lisette went last year to a school near Paris. In September she goes to a school in London. An American who lives in a small house below comes each day to tutor her."

Claudine brought us fluffy omelets and fresh-from-the-oven croissants. I hadn't touched breakfast on the plane. Now I relished the meal set before us. We lingered over second cups of coffee while Dad talked about my going with him to Copenhagen for an overnight stay.

"It is a quick flight. You will enjoy seeing Copenhagen while I transact my business. Now finish up your coffee and go up to your room to sleep," he said briskly. "I will see that no one disturbs you. Come down when you are awake and fully rested."

Without Dad's telling me I knew my room had been redone in anticipation of my arrival. The room was decorated in the pleasingly uncluttered fashion that I had seen downstairs. The furniture was Mediterranean and the walls were an orange-gold. The casement windows and the French doors that led to the balcony had butter-yellow draperies. I crossed to a window, pushed it wide to allow in the crisp morning air.

I made no effort to unpack, except to pull out a pair of pajamas. I changed with utter exhaustion, turned down the bed, and slid beneath the cover, eager for sleep.

* * *

I came awake slowly, conscious of the sunlight that poured through the casement window I had opened earlier. I was pleasurably aware of my surroundings. Outside my windows the magnificent view of Lake Geneva, the Alps beyond. Right now it was enough to know that it was there.

I stretched beneath the covers, giving myself up to sloth. My eyes shut against the sunlight; I was content just to be. Then quite suddenly, a voice drifted up through the open window. It was a cultured, feminine, British voice, speaking agitatedly.

"Armand, I don't know what to make of you," she was saying, her voice faintly strident. Instinctively I knew this was my grandmother. "How can you let this girl take you in so completely? She's a clever young opportunist taking advantage of a similarity of names! Somehow she found out about your earlier marriage. She's plotted this whole thing because she knows you're a rich man. All she wants is to share your money, Armand! She's a phony!"

Chapter Three

I tossed aside the coverlet and crossed barefoot, trembling, to the window. I was drawn compulsively to the voices below.

"Maman, please understand," Dad was pleading. "It was one of those one-in-a-million encounters. She *is* Andrea. My Andrea. I spoke with her mother on the telephone."

"And after all these years you recognized her voice?" The tone was scathing. "Really, Armand, how can you be so gullible? It was all set up ahead of time. Every detail planned to seem real."

"How could Andrea have known I would be at the Svedborg's party? I was not sure myself until the last moment that I would go. No," he said positively, "this is my child."

"Armand, please, check this out," she urged. "I'm so sure this is some horrendous fraud. I don't want to see you hurt."

"All right," he said after a moment, and suddenly my heart was pounding. "I will make inquiries."

But he knew I was his daughter. He was making inquiries only to prove this to his mother. How could there be two Andrea Lavals with mothers named Marcy? Dad spoke to Mother on the phone. Even after all these years, he wouldn't forget her voice.

I stood at the window, staring out at the beauty before me. The tiers of lush green vineyards, occasionally broken by clusters of modest houses that were tiny villages. Here and there the red and white of a Swiss flag. The incredible blue of the vast lake, where the sun glinted off a paddle boat moving toward Lausanne. The mountains opposite were now less sharply etched than this morning, their peaks seemingly lost in the clouds. But I saw all this with only a part of my mind.

How could I prove my identity? Suddenly it was urgent to prove it beyond a doubt. Sit down this minute. Write a letter to the Board of Health in New York City, where I was born. Ask for a copy of the long form birth certificate. The birth certificate I used to obtain my passport was the short form, pertaining only to me. The long form would list Armand Laval as my father. *Wouldn't it?* I'd never seen the long form.

A barrage of questions assaulted my mind. Did my grandmother honestly believe I was a phony, out to share the Laval money? Or was she rebelling at accepting the child of her son's first wife? Was she automatically hostile about anything concerning that first marriage? Mother said she had insisted it was a mistake.

Fleetingly I toyed with the idea of making a transatlantic call to my mother to put her on the phone with my grandmother. But that would be melodramatic. I must be cool about this. My grandmother would never forgive melodrama.

I would write to the New York Board of Health right now. Would it take them long to get the certificate back to me? I would stress the urgency, pray for speed. I opened a suitcase to bring out a pants suit, decided to unpack completely before I wrote the letter. It would take only ten minutes and save pressing time later.

With my wardrobe, exuberantly chosen for the expected fifteen days in Scandinavia, hung away or stashed in the expansive drawer space of the elegant double dresser and matching chest, I changed into the Persian blue pants suit, and slid my feet into sandals.

Now I sat down to the write the letter. Drop a note to Mother, too, I ordered myself. She'd expect to hear. She was avid for details about my month at the chateau. I dug out my packet of airmail stationery, sat down to write the two letters. Both brief. At a piano downstairs someone was playing "Clair de Lune." Playing brilliantly. Surely not Lisette?

28

The letters written, I found envelopes, addressed each, enclosed the letters and with the Board of Health letter a check I was certain would cover costs. I remembered, as I slid both envelopes into my jacket pocket, the post office we'd passed in Bougy Villars. A brisk ten minute walk each way, I calculated. No more. And with that marvelous scenery, the walk would be a pleasure.

At the door, I paused, gearing myself for the confrontation with my grandmother. With Lisette. With my hand on the knob, I forced a smile. I wasn't supposed to know of my grandmother's skepticism. I was sure she was too polite to indicate this face to face. But I knew.

I walked out into the upstairs hall. The piano was silent. From somewhere on the lower floor came the staccato sound of rapid typing. That would be Pat Fraser. Where was Dad now? Panic touched me. I wanted him there when I first met my grandmother.

My mother's parents had both died before I was born. Dad's father was dead. The English lady who had spoken so harshly of my identity was my sole surviving grandparent. It could have been a poignant meeting.

I left my room, still wearing a set smile. How did you respond to a grandmother who mentally disowned you? Go on, Andrea, don't dawdle.

Again, as I started down the stairs, I heard someone at the piano. The music obviously unfamiliar to whoever sat before the keyboard. Again, it was Debussy.

At the foot of the stairs I halted, conscious of my inner tensions, the way my heart pounded. No! Be casual. Let no one realize I was afraid of meeting my grandmother and sister. It could be an exhilarating experience. Just as finding Dad had been. *Would* it?

"Andrea—" Dad stood in a doorway far up the hall as I swung in the direction of the music. His smile was warm, reassuring. "You did not sleep as long as I expected." A gentle reproach in his voice.

"I feel great." I tried to sound convincing. "It was all the rest I needed."

"Come in here and met Pat Fraser," he ordered, and turned to smile at someone inside the room as I approached. "Pat, here is Andrea."

Pat Fraser sat at a desk by the window and swung her

29

chair around so that she faced me. She was a plain woman except for genuinely beautiful champagne blonde hair that swept to her shoulders in a fashion that was too young for her. It was incongruous somehow with the primness of her face. Mid-forties, I suspected, and terrific at her job.

"Hello, Andrea," she said with a reserve that I knew would not easily be worn down. "Welcome to Switzerland."

"Thank you." At least Pat Fraser wasn't hostile. She was waiting for me to prove myself.

"Come, Andrea," Dad said with a glow of anticipation. "Your grandmother and Lisette are in the library." Suddenly he halted. "Here comes Heidi to welcome you."

A massive St. Bernard with huge brown eyes, her fur magnificently brushed, ambled good-humoredly towards us.

"Oh, she's beautiful!" I adore all dogs and Heidi was especially impressive. "Hello, Heidi." I leaned forward with affection to caress the huge silken head.

"You've made a friend." Dad chuckled as a wet tongue slithered forward to brush my cheek. "Heidi is usually more reserved than this." Clearly he was pleased with my conquest.

With Dad's arm about my waist and Heidi leading us, we turned in at the doorway a few feet ahead. Lisette sat at the piano, frowning slightly as she struggled to play a difficult passage. She was a lovely little girl with soft, near-black hair that fell almost to her waist in a silken sweep. She looked much like the painting of Michel, which hung in the hall. They had been, I remembered, twins.

Lisette leaned earnestly over the keyboard, not yet aware of our presence.

"Maman," Dad said with a faint tone of command in his voice, and the tall, slender, white-haired woman at the window turned around. Even now, when she was probably seventy, she showed signs of beauty. Her features had sharpened with age, but were still cameo-like. Her head was held high and her hair was beautifully coiffed. She was seemingly in superb control, but I saw the anger in her dark eyes when she forced herself to look at me. "Here is Andrea, Maman." He was uncomfortable, guarded.

"It will take us a while to get to know each other, Andrea," she said coolly, making no move to come to me. The reserve in her voice restraining me from any impulsive overture of affection. "Welcome to Chateau Laval." A dryness in her voice said that she was certain I was here because the Laval family was rich.

"Thank you." Polite and impersonal. Not yet accepting that this elegant older woman was my grandmother.

Lisette, who had broken off from her piano playing, sat watching us. And then, in a burst of exuberance, she was darting across the room to throw herself against me.

"Andrea, it's wonderful! Just wonderful to have a grown sister! I'm so glad Father found you!"

She pulled away to gaze up into my face. Her face was pink with excitement, her eyes shining. Oh, now I felt welcomed! How ingratiating, how pretty she was. My small sister. Dad beamed at us, delighted with this unexpected reaction from Lisette. I'd thought I'd have to win her over slowly.

"I think it's wonderful, too, Lisette," I said, pulling her face to mine.

And then there was a moment of constrained silence, though for Lisette it seemed enough to gaze at me while she held onto my hands. I sensed that Dad was upset at my grandmother's polite but cold response.

"Andrea, you have letters in your pocket," Lisette said pertly. "Would you like to go down to the post office to mail them? We can bike down. There are two bikes."

"Lisette, do not drag her away so quickly," Dad reproached laughingly, but I felt my grandmother's relief at this possibility.

"Will you come, Andrea?" Lisette persuaded impetuously.

"If it's all right." I looked inquiringly at Dad. I was making a point of not gazing directly at my grandmother.

"Go ahead," Dad capitulated. "We will not sit down to lunch for perhaps an hour."

Lisette clung to my arm, prodding me towards the rear of the house. Savory aromas emerged from the kitchen as we approached.

"Jeanne," Lisette called out ingenuously at the kitchen door. "This is my sister." She turned to me. "Jeanne likes for me to speak with her in English so that she can practice the language. And, of course, Grandmère prefers that we speak English."

31

"Hello, Jeanne." I smiled at the pretty, dark-haired girl, probably still in her teens.

"It is so nice for Lisette to have a sister." Jeanne radiated friendliness. All the staff, I realized, must know the story of my sudden emergence as a member of the family. To Jeanne this was a true Cinderella story.

"Nice for me, too," I said, hugging Lisette. How small and fragile she was! But in another year or two, like my other youngest half sister, she would be as tall as I.

"Come with me to the bikes," Lisette coaxed.

Claudine turned away from the range where she had been stirring the contents of an iron casserole.

"Do not be late for luncheon, Lisette," she warned sternly in French. "I will not hold up the meal." Briefly her eyes met mine. I felt chilled.

Lisette and I collected the two bicycles at a small rack to the right of the kitchen, walked them down the driveway, down the steep incline to the road that would take us to the post office.

We pedaled slowly in the noonday sun, pleased with each other's company.

"There's Larry!" Lisette braked the bike, pointed to a sun-bather sprawled on a cot before a pink house set at the edge of a vineyard. "Oh, he's asleep." She was disappointed. "I wanted you to meet him."

"I'll meet him later," I cajoled. "Who is he?" Tall, sandy-haired, already tan, with the casual good looks—from this distance—that you encounter in cigarette ads.

"Larry Woods, the American who lives with Phillipe Nicolet. He's my tutor this summer. The rest of the year he teaches English at a school in Geneva. Phillipe also works at the school." Her eyes were reflective as she smiled. "Michel likes Larry and Phillipe, too. Almost as much as I do." I turned to her with a start. Michel had been dead six years. "I play a game," Lisette explained. "Michel is alive. Only nobody can see him except me. That way I am not so lonely. But now I have you." She leaned forward impetuously, taking one hand from the handle bars to place it on mine. "Andrea, you *will* stay for the whole month, won't you?"

"I'll stay." I was touched by her eagerness.

"You must say nothing to Grandmère about the game I

32

play with Michel. She becomes very angry with me. Our secret?" What an ingratiating smile, I thought with a surge of affection. How wonderful to have found Dad and Lisette. I could tolerate a disbelieving grandmother.

"Our secret," I said hastily because Lisette was gazing at me with incipient alarm.

"Michel loves to bike, but he hates practicing the piano. But I practice enough for both of us." She squinted in thought, her head pertly to one side. "Grandmère is your Grandmère, too, isn't she?" What a somber assessment.

"Yes, she is, Lisette."

"Sometimes it's hard to like Grandmère when you first meet her. But you'll like her later, Andrea. You'll see," she promised with optimism.

Would I? Wistfully, I wished that I could.

"Henri is fierce sometimes, but he's my friend," Lisette confided complacently. "Sometimes he's sad because he has no children. Then we pretend I'm his daughter. Don't mind that he hates Americans." Suddenly Lisette was perturbed. "It's because of what happened long ago. Before we were even born," she said solemnly.

"What happened, Lisette?" I felt compelled to ask. Besides, Lisette waited avidly for the question.

"It was after World War II. Henri was to marry a girl in his village. Instead, she ran off to America to marry a soldier she'd met during the war. She never said a word to him," Lisette went on dramatically, reliving a no doubt off-repeated story. "But all the time she was planning. Then one day she just left. I heard Father talk about it, and Claudine." She smiled shyly. "I was in the United States. Did you know?"

"No." I turned to her with bright-eyed inquiry. "When?"

"During the school holidays last spring. I begged and begged, and finally Father said, yes, I could go there with my roommate from school, who comes from the States. Grandmère was furious."

"Where did you visit?"

"New York. The television was marvelous. We watched every chance we got." Her eyes were wistful. "I have to keep remembering not to talk about it to Henri. Even now he hates to hear about America."

In the village the houses were shuttered against the noon-

33

day sun. Not an inhabitant in view except for a pair of toddlers who played in a doorway with a small, frolicking kitten. The one store was shut tightly for the lunch hour.

As we approached the tiny, modern post office, I dug into my pocket for francs that had been part of the "tip pack" I'd bought back in New York at Manufacturers Hanover. But the post office door was shut. A sign briefed us on the hours when the post office was open.

Lisette stared in consternation.

"I thought it would be open. We never go to the post office," she acknowledged with winsome apology. "Always the mail is put into the box, and the postman picks it up."

"Never mind," I soothed. "Probably Pat has stamps in her desk. We'll ask her later."

But the post office hours intrigued me. It was open from 6:45 A.M. to 9:00 A.M., then closed until 1:30 P.M. While the postman delivered the mail, I wondered humorously? It was reopened from 1:30 to 3:00 P.M., closed again until 5:30 P.M., when it opened again for an hour. What an intricate schedule for a tiny, picturesque village which wore an aura of centuries past.

Lisette and I explored the town until the point where the road took a sharp downward incline to another tier around the side of the mountain. Then we turned around and started to pedal slowly back towards the chateau, stopping en route to read the date on a watering trough that offered a bright display of petunias.

"Look at the date, Lisette." I leaned forward, gazed with respect. "1798!" Forgetting that this was comparatively recent for Europe.

We stopped again to sit on a bench outside a small church that was a magnificent observation point, until Lisette reached for my wrist to check the time.

"We had better go," Lisette said with a small sigh of regret. "Claudine will be furious if we're not there when lunch is ready to be served." She paused, frowning in thought for an instant. "But Claudine has been with Grandmère for thirty years. That's a long time, isn't it?"

"Long," I agreed. Claudine could be forgiven some idiosyncracies. "Come," I ordered lightly. "I'll race you back to the chateau."

We could hear Claudine talking sharply to Jeanne as we

put the bikes back in the rack and sauntered into the house. Was Claudine always this sharp, or was it my presence that put her teeth on edge? Did everybody who knew my father suspect me of being an adventuress? I hadn't even known he was wealthy until he picked me up in the chauffeured Bentley! United Nations people are not usually rich and I associated him with the others.

We skirted the kitchen, walked down the hall towards the family dining room, hearing the rapid beat of Pat Fraser's typewriter. The table was laid for lunch. Elegant and attractive. Grandmère was at the buffet, arranging a low vase of roses, larkspur, lilies, and native orchids. A, task she seemingly enjoyed.

"Grandmère, the post office was not open," Lisette reported. "Isn't that strange?"

Grandmère frowned, turned to us with an effort to conceal her irritation.

"They have their schedule in the village," she said crisply. "It is not for us to criticize. We are only holiday people." She stared at the hem of Lisette's white slacks. "Lisette, you have grease from the bicycle on your slacks again. Go upstairs and change quickly. In a few moments luncheon will be served." Now she turned to me. I knew it was an effort even to address impersonal words directly to me. "Andrea, will you please go down the hall to the office and tell Pat that Jeanne will serve in a few moments. She never thinks to look at a clock."

"I'll tell her." I was relieved to escape. Absurdly I thought of Betty Lynne and her "bad vibrations." This kind of hostility gave me "bad vibrations." It was going to be difficult to live here for a whole month, with such hostility surrounding me. But Dad and Lisette were glad that I was here. Forget the others.

I paused at the open door to the office, told Pat that lunch was about to be served.

"Thank you." Her smile impersonally polite, but not hostile. "I'll tell Monsieur Laval." Not "I'll tell your father." "I'll tell Monsieur Laval." Only my father and Lisette genuinely believed I was Armand Laval's daughter.

I dawdled before the portrait of Michel, stalling my return to the dining room. He was such a handsome little boy. My brother—and I'd never known him. I felt a startling sense of loss. What an awful shock to Dad when Michel and his mother died. A boating accident, Dad said. How had it happened?

I must go back into the dining room, I told myself uncomfortably. Force myself to make small talk with my grandmother. For Dad's sake I must try to make a friend of her. Could I, I asked myself skeptically? Ever?

Mother, who was garrulous on practically every subject, had been reticent about discussing her first marriage. Over the phone it had been difficult to probe. All she had cared to do was to vindicate herself for lying to me about Dad.

Had something happened between my mother and grandmother to bring on this hostility? Certain that this was caused by more than her suspicion that I wasn't, in reality, her son's daughter.

"Andrea—"

I spun about to face my father, managing a smile.

"I've been inspecting the paintings," I improvised.

"Come on with me to the dining room," he invited.

Pat Fraser moved past him, headed with long, impatient steps for the dining room. She had a tight control about her that I suspected concealed a passionate nature. She would be a dangerous adversary.

Dad reached out a hand to me as I approached. I gave him mine. Together we started towards the dining room. But first I spied Lisette, racing down the wide stairway. A brilliant smile on her face for me. Dad and Lisette were on my side, I thought with a surge of defiance. I was not alone at the Chateau Laval.

Lunch, as I'd anticipated, was a gourmet delight. Table conversation was, on the surface, casual and pleasant. But I found it impossible to relax, to enjoy the delicious patè, the breaded escalope of veal, the fluffy potatoes, the salad, the chocolate mousse that was just right—not over-sweet.

Dad launched into a discussion of his projected trip to Copenhagen. I noticed the astonishment on Pat's face when he mentioned he was taking me along. She was annoyed. No matter, I told myself defensively. It was no concern of hers.

I relished going to yet another foreign country. How casually Europeans could travel from one country to another —the way we in the United States travel from one state to another. I made a swift mental calculation. We would just miss being in Copenhagen when Kathy and Betty Lynne would be there.

When lunch was over, everyone headed for the second floor bedrooms.

"It is the custom here to rest after lunch, Andrea," Dad explained. "And in the heat of the summer this is a good practice."

I returned to my room after an impulsive hug from Lisette, en route to her own, with one small hand entrenched in her father's. I closed the door, crossed to the chest of drawers where I'd stashed away several paperbacks I'd brought along for vacation reading.

I opened the drawer, debating in my mind about which mystery to read first. And then I froze in shock. My eyes fastened to the contents of the drawer. The drawer which I had neatly arranged only two hours ago, was now in utter disorder. I stared with a surge of fury, instinct ordering me to inspect further. Every drawer of the chest, of the dresser, was a shambles.

Who had been in my room? Who had gone through my possessions with a vicious disregard for order?

My heart pounding, I strode across the room to my closet. Pulled the door wide. Everything I'd hung neatly on hangers lay in one huddle on the floor.

Atop the pile of rumpled clothes one dress caught my eye. A long dinner dress I'd extravagantly bought because Kathy insisted we should be prepared for a possible festive occasion. The gaily printed silk had been ruthlessly slashed in a dozen places. I would never wear it.

I thought about the voodoo dolls associated with the primitives of some islands in the West Indies. And I knew. This was my voodoo doll. Someone slashing my best dress. Pretending I was inside. *Wishing me dead.*

37

Chapter Four

My hands unsteady. I reached for the slashed dress, pulled one of my suitcases from the corner of the closet, and thrust the dress inside. Feeling sick as I zipped the suitcase closed again. Fighting down my instinct to dash from the room, to seek out Dad and tell him what had happened.

No! I mustn't tell Dad. Don't highlight this hostility towards me. I must cope with this myself somehow. I won't be driven away from the chateau. This is my father's house. He wants me here. Nobody is going to frighten me away.

In an aura of unreality, battling for calm, I set about rehanging the jumbles of dresses, pantsuits and coats on the floor. Then I moved to the dresser to reorganize the disordered drawers.

What could I do to protect myself from another such intrusion? There *would* be another. I shivered faintly, almost feeling the shears that had slashed my dress coming at my throat. For a moment—only a moment—I considered packing up and leaving.

I abandoned the drawer on which I was working to cross to the door, involved now with the need to protect myself. I bent to inspect the lock. A simple key lock; the kind for which a pass key can be bought in any hardware store.

All right, I promised myself defiantly. The next time the intruder came—and instinct told me that there would be another time—the door would be locked.

I would have to take one small gamble on time, I judged. I'd have to leave the door unlocked until Jeanne did my bedroom. For the rest of the day—and the night—my door would be locked. Nobody would know; only the person who tried to intrude again.

I went back and finished the rearrangement of the drawers. My mind focused on acquiring a key. The nearest town was Aubonne. Surely I could find a hardware store there. Dad said we were about two kilometers from Aubonne. I could walk or bike there. Alone, I cautioned myself, so that I could go into a hardware store to buy a key.

With my room once again in order, I dug into my purse for the Swiss money provided by my "tip pack," slid coins and bills into the pocket of my jacket. Unhappy that the door could not be locked now, I left the room conscious of the heavy afternoon stillness that pervaded. A stillness that was suddenly menacing. Noiselessly I walked down the stairs, cut around to the rear hall.

Jeanne, Claudine, and Henri were having their lunch at a large square table in the kitchen. Both Claudine and Henri looked up with annoyance at my approach. Was it Claudine, or Henri, who had so viciously slashed my dress? Nothing in their eyes told me. Could it have been some psychotic stranger who wandered into the chateau? *Why?*

Deliberately, I ignored Claudine and Henri, spoke to Jeanne. It was Jeanne, I remembered defensively, who enjoyed practicing her English.

"I'm taking a bike and going to Aubonne," I said with contrived casualness. "How do I get there?"

"Oh, it is easy, Mademoiselle," Jeanne said eagerly. "Just go down the steep hill to the first road. Make a left. That will take you directly into Aubonne."

"Thank you, Jeanne."

I pedalled down the hill to the narrow stone-fenced road.

The sun was Riviera hot. The vineyards apparently deserted at this hour. Perhaps, I decided, the work was done for the season. They waited now for the miles of grapes to ripen sufficiently for picking. Wine grapes, I assumed.

I pedalled along the lightly populated road with a sense of adventure watching the cars, which appeared to be miniatures at this altitude, race along the auto-route below. The traffic never seemed to be heavy, I thought, mentally comparing it to the major arteries around New York City.

When the houses began to sit on tiny suburban-type

plots, I realized I was approaching Aubonne. A small town, but there surely would be a hardware store. It was absurd, I knew, to place such security in acquiring a key. Yet I had a compulsion to guarantee myself this slight protection.

I pedalled through the arch that led into the town, turned down the steep, narrow, cobbled road between one-person-wide sidewalks. Small shops topped by apartments with luxuriantly planted window boxes lined the streets.

Down below, in a miniscule parking area before the post-office, I parked the bike and began to stroll about smiling at a couple that, like me, were obviously tourists, and delighted with the quaint, Old World quality of the town.

I inspected the jewelry store window, admired the clocks, moved on to the mouth-watering display in the bakery shop window next door. On impulse I walked into the bakery, bought cookies to take back to Lisette, enjoying the small exchange with the charming girl behind the counter and delighted to discover my French was adequate.

At the girl's direction I left the bakery and cut across the parking area to the street beyond, where I found a hardware store. Like the girl in the bakery, the people here were eager to be helpful. For a franc I bought my key.

I dawdled another half hour, gazing into the small stores, stopping in the drugstore to buy suntan lotion because the bike ride into town had reminded me this would be essential.

At the chateau, I put the bike back into the rack, went inside. Claudine and Henri were arguing in rapid, angry French. Both stopped dead at my approach. But not before one sentence etched itself on my mind.

I smiled politely and continued on my way. My heart hammering. What did Henri mean when he said, "The girl will cause trouble"?

The door to the rooms used as the office suite was closed. I could hear Dad inside, dictating to Pat. I started up the stairs. From behind a closed door came the sound of a record player. Lisette playing pop music in her room, singing along in a surprisingly sweet, childish soprano.

I knocked lightly at the door. Lisette opened it with a quick smile. Heidi's huge head pushed forward to be patted.

"I biked to Aubonne," I explained. "I brought you some cookies."

"Oh, thank you, Andrea." She reached enthusiastically for the small bag, then frowned as she held it tightly in one hand. "Don't tell Grandmère. She hates me to eat between meals."

"I won't," I promised guiltily. I hadn't thought to ask permission. It had been a spontaneous wish to please.

"Would you like to listen with me to my records?" Andrea invited.

"Some other time, Lisette. I have to unpack now," I fabricated. "I'll see you later."

Inside my room I pulled the key from my jacket pocket and self-consciously inserted it in the lock. I held my breath as I turned it. It worked! The door was locked.

I left the key in position. Anyone trying to get past that lock must first knock the key from its position. I'm a light sleeper. Such a sound would most likely waken me.

I yawned; I felt tired. The bed was suddenly strongly inviting. The nap I'd taken earlier was insufficient to recompense me for the lost night of sleep.

I set the alarm, knowing I might just sleep through the night, ignoring dinner, without some jarring insistence that I awake.

I reached for my travel clock, set the alarm, and gave myself up to sleep—sleep that was spiked with uneasy dreams. I came awake with a start, reached to quiet the noisy small monster on my night table. I struggled into a semi-sitting position. What had I been dreaming? Nothing complete in my mind. Only disquieting fragments.

Dinner would be served late, I recalled. I had much time on my hands before it would be necessary to go downstairs. Suddenly I was assaulted by a need to schedule this time. Soak in a tub. Brush aside this painful tension that made my shoulder blades ache. Make a production of dressing for dinner. Look my best, my first night in the chateau.

Leaning over the tub to adjust the water, I all at once froze. What was that? That sound at my door. Had someone tried to come in and discovered the door was locked?

Kicking off my low, walking shoes I moved noiselessly into the bedroom, stared at the door. No sign of the knob moving. But I spied something on the floor, just inside the door. Something which had not been there earlier.

Slowly I walked to the door and bent to pick up the sheet

41

of white typewriter paper. Letters cut from a newspaper, had been pasted to the sheet of paper. "American, go home. Or die."

Fury taking precedence over caution, I unlocked the door, charged into the corridor. My heart pounding as I gazed in first one direction, then the other. No one in sight. I was alone.

Trembling, I walked back into the room and locked the door again. I reread the ugly message in my hand, not actually believing, then, that someone would try to kill me. I was furious at this psychotic threat. Still, fear infiltrated me. Who had slipped this beneath my door? Except for the residents of the chateau, no one was aware of my presence in the area.

Now words ticker-taped across my mind. Lisette's words, telling me about Henri, who hated Americans. Had Henri thrust this note under my door? No, I mustn't condemn him without more convincing grounds than Lisette's story of Henri's thwarted romance.

I couldn't bring myself to tell Dad about the slashed dress. But this note I would show him. I could be casual about this on the surface. It was no secret that in many parts of Europe Americans are not warmly welcomed. Dad would know how to track down whoever sent this note. I wouldn't be bothered again, I decided optimistically.

I deposited the sheet of paper on the dresser and went into the bathroom. Almost defiantly, I reached into a drawer for my jar of bath salts and dumped the yellow crystals extravagantly into the steaming water. For a little while, with the door to my room locked against intruders, I would be able to relax.

Less than twenty hours before I had been drinking coffee at JFK with Kathy and Betty Lynne. It seemed a century ago.

* * *

I inspected my reflection in the mirror. There were faint circles beneath my eyes. That was to be expected after my flight and my lack of sleep. But I saw no fear there. I must not let anybody believe I was afraid. Particularly not the person who had slid that note beneath my door while I slept.

42

I reached for the note, folded it over small enough to cup in one hand. Take it to Dad. Let him be on guard. Somebody in this elegant chateau wished me dead.

As I walked downstairs, I could hear Lisette romping outdoors with Heidi. Her grandmother was calling to her from a window.

"Lisette, please, not so much noise."

I remembered now that Dad said Grandmère had a phobia about noise. The television, Lisette's record player, must always be played at low volume.

No sounds of typing now. Pat must be upstairs in her room. Was Grandmère's coldness towards Pat based partly on her dislike of the sound of typing?

Savory aromas permeated the lower floor. Claudine talked to Jeanne, rather more loudly than necessary. Something about which dishes to use on the table.

I walked down the hall to the library and peered inside. Dad sat in a black leather club chair, absorbed in a Geneva newspaper.

"Will I disturb you if I come in?" I asked lightly, but the palms of my hands were clammy.

Dad glanced up with a smile of welcome.

"Come sit here with me, Andrea." Immediately, he discarded the newspaper and rose to his feet. "Would you like a glass of sherry? Dinner won't be served for at least half an hour. Claudine is temperamental when she serves duck. We must sit down at precisely the right moment."

"Yes, I'd like a sherry, please." Gear myself with sherry to play this with the matter-of-factness I didn't feel.

Dad crossed to the bar, poured two glasses of sherry with an air of pleasure at our having these few minutes alone.

"I have not shown you the photograph of you in my wallet," he said reminiscently. He handed me my glass of sherry, set his own aside with an air of conspiracy, and reached into his pocket for his wallet. "It was all I had of you. Several years ago it began to fade. I had a fresh negative and new prints made."

Dad opened the wallet, handed it to me. Eagerly I gazed at the photograph of a serious-eyed toddler of about fifteen months.

"I've never seen this one."

I concentrated on the snapshot of me, visualizing Dad all

43

those years ago when he had taken this. Feeling such a rush of love when I considered his shock when Mother disappeared with me that way.

"For twenty years, Andrea, this photograph was all I had of my daughter." His eyes were anguished with recall. "On your birthdays I was unbearable. I kept away from everyone. But now," he said with optimism, "it is all over. Your next birthday we will spend together. Even if I have to fly to New York to spend it with you."

"I'll hold you to that," I warned. The sharp edges of the folded-over paper were digging into my moist palm. Reminding me of what I must say. "Oh, something—something strange happened." I fumbled for the right word. Something in the tone of my voice, despite my effort at casualness, betraying my unease. "I found this under my door when I came out of my bath." I held out the sheet of paper with its pasted-up message.

With a look of concern Dad took the paper, spread it wide while I forced myself to sip the excellent sherry Dad had poured for me. I saw his initial shock, followed by a controlled fury.

"Who could do a thing like this?" He rose to his feet. Scowling at the pasted-up sheet in his hand. "There has never been anti-American feelings in this neighborhood. These are fine, country people, Andrea. They live quiet, good lives." He frowned in thought for a moment, then crossed to the door.

"Henri!" he called out loudly. "Henri!"

Dad came back into the room, reached for his sherry glass, with his free hand thrusting the ugly paper into his jacket pocket.

"Tomorrow I will speak with the police in both Bougy Villars and Aubonne. It is the tourist season. There are strangers coming into the area for a day, perhaps for a week. They must keep an eye on these people," he said sternly.

Henri walked into the room with a look of inquiry.

"*Monsieur?*" he asked politely.

"Henri, I wish you to make certain from now on that all doors to the chateau are kept locked. Day and night," he emphasized. "Please tell Claudine and Jeanne. At night you will lock all lower floor shutters."

"*Oui, Monsieur.*" His eyes polite but startled. Was that

camouflage? Was it Henri, notoriously anti-American, who had placed that note under my door? Who had slashed my dress so viciously?

"That is all, Henri," Dad dismissed him. "But please remember."

"Oui, Monsieur." Henri nodded firmly and left us.

"Andrea, I am furious about this." His eyes held mine with apology. "What a dreadful welcome!"

"I know it's just some crackpot. I'm not upset," I lied, striving for amused nonchalance.

"Normally the Swiss are most security minded," Dad said. "Lower floor windows are heavily shuttered and locked at night. Windows without shutters have iron grills. At first glance you might believe they are decorative. Believe me, they are there for utilitarian purposes. This amused me when we first bought the house because it seemed to me so ridiculous, in the midst of all this openness, this beauty, to be alarmed about burglars."

"I was astonished to find that note under my door." But I had not suspected an outsider.

"It is so simple to gain entry into the house. Doors are always open, even at night. But no more," Dad promised grimly. "We'll stop this intrusion."

Dad was convinced a stranger had come into the house to place that note under my door. *Because he didn't know about the slashed dress.* I considered briefly confiding in him about this, then childishly backed away. No, Dad wouldn't believe that someone in the chateau had been responsible for that madness. He was too close to everyone. Too trusting. He would believe this, too, was an act of a stranger.

"Monsieur Laval—" Pat hurried into a room, a letter in her hand. "You forgot to sign this one." She stiffened at the sight of me and color stained her cheeks.

Pat Fraser was furious with me for coming into the chateau, I realized with a surge of discomfort. Up until now she'd concealed this behind a facade of politeness. She resented the love between Dad and me because she was in love with Dad.

Dad signed the letter, returned it to Pat, and she went back to the office. Somewhere, not more than a hundred

45

yards distant, there was a sudden, sharp report like that of a gun. I started. My eyes swept involuntarily to Dad in alarm.

"Firecrackers," Dad explained. "Tomorrow is Swiss Independence Day. In Bougy Villars and in Aubonne the bands will play. The flags will be hung out. And the firecrackers will sound off. Your grandmother will be very irritable," he cautioned gently, "because she hates the noise. Like Heidi, who hides beneath a bed."

Earlier than Dad expected, Henri arrived to announce that dinner was about to be served. As we headed towards the dining room, we heard Grandmère talking with Lisette on the stairs, also en route to the dining room. Pat was already seated, wearing a severely simple, unrelieved black dress. Her hands were folded in her lap, her eyes fastened to the low vase of flowers. As we approached, she glanced up with a faint inscrutable smile.

"Grandmère, I talked with Larry this afternoon," Lisette reported ingenuously over the delicious leek soup. "I invited him to come early tomorrow and swim in the pool." Her eyes moved impishly to me. Lisette was impatient for me to meet their American neighbor.

"Was that necessary?" Grandmère's voice was sharp.

"No, but I thought it would be fun." Lisette's eyes were wide with innocence that was suspect. Her bright little mind was conniving.

"Really, she should clear these invitations through me," Grandmère objected querulously.

"Maman, so he comes early to swim," Dad chided. "I have told him, and Phillipe as well, to use the pool whenever they like. What does it matter?"

"Tomorrow may I go to hear the band play again?" Lisette turned eagerly to Pat. "Remember last year, Pat? You took me with you."

"If your grandmother agrees, Lisette, of course you may come with me again," Pat said carefully. Her affection for Lisette shone through, but discretion forced her to defer to Grandmère.

Dad punctured the heavy silence that fell about us with talk about Geneva, which he promised to show to me as soon as he was caught up with business.

"I think Geneva is a cold city," Pat said frankly in reply

to a question from Dad. For a moment she was disconcert-ed by this revelation, until she saw Dad's grin of concurr-ence.

"Like a cold, beautiful woman," Dad said. Involuntarily my eyes swept to my grandmother. Beautiful, still, and cold —or terribly controlled. For a moment our eyes clashed. Did she honestly believe I was an imposter? "There are times," he insisted, "when Geneva is the most beautiful city in the world." Now he frowned slightly. His mind traitor-ously backtracking, I guessed, to the moment when I'd handed him the note I'd found under my door. He was dis-turbed.

Henri served Claudine's superb duck with wine sauce. The string bean salad, the roast potatoes were the perfect complements. Tired as I was, unnerved as I was, I ate with relish, knowing this was gourmet cuisine such as I rarely encountered.

Dessert was a deliciously flaky strawberry tart. Grandmère had a piece of fresh fruit instead. I remem-bered, guiltily, the cookies I'd bought for Lisette in Au-bonne. Grandmère would be annoyed if she knew. Covertly I inspected her, wishing she would allow me to feel affec-tion, chafing at the wall she kept between us.

Immediately after dinner Dad insisted I go up to bed.

"With a good night's rest," he said gently, "you will be back to normal. No more jet lag."

I was relieved to go to my room. Tiredness had begun to creep over me again along with dessert. But I was upset when Lisette rose from the table to tag along with me. How would it look when, at my door, I bent down to pull the key to my room from my shoe?

Lisette chattered gaily as we climbed the stairs, while I searched my mind for a way out of this small predicament. At the top of the stairs I playfully reached for Lisette's hand.

"Come," I said affectionately, "I'll walk you to your room. Which is it?"

"Next to yours," Lisette said, pleased with this small game.

At her door I kissed her goodnight, closed the door be-hind her. As I moved away I heard her talking to Heidi, who was banished to Lisette's room for the night. At my

47

door I stooped to fish the key from my shoe. I unlocked the door, let myself inside, reached to flip on the light switch, and locked the door again, leaving the key in place.

I crossed to the French doors which opened onto the small balcony, intent on drawing the draperies tight against the night. I gasped in amazement at the beauty before me.

The lake lay clothed in darkness except for a wide swathe of moonlit water. The lights of France, on the other side of the lake were dazzling miles of brilliance that swept as far as I could see. To my right Geneva. To my left the lights of Morges and Lausanne.

Far below the headlights of the cars made the auto-route a mammoth, diamond-encrusted bracelet. Seemingly parallel, there were the lights of a night train en route to Lausanne. Closer, in the midst of the expanse of the vineyards, were the lights from the clusters of modest houses that formed the villages.

Yet standing here on the narrow balcony I felt the cold wind of fear. Hastily I stepped inside, pulled the doors shut. The night was warm but I locked the French doors, crossed to shut and lock the windows, one by one, and pulled the draperies tight against the outside darkness.

Only now did I feel secure. A surface security. Despite my tiredness, I lay awake for an interminable time.

Chapter Five

I awoke to a glorious, sunny morning, crossed to the windows to open the draperies and gaze out upon my perfect view. This morning there was a slight haze across the mountain peaks. Mont Blanc was in hiding.

On a tier below a slow process of army vehicles moved along. This evidence of the military was incongruous in such a tranquil atmosphere. But I remembered that every Swiss male is trained to bear arms, though the country has been an island of peace for well over a hundred years.

I glanced at the clock. Just 9:30 but already the day promised to be hot. The pool, I guessed, would be icy from the night drop in temperature, not warming until afternoon. Lisette's last words to me before I told her goodnight had been to remind me of my promise to join her in the pool. She was plotting to introduce me to Larry Woods. Already a romantic at twelve, I thought tenderly.

All right, fortify myself with coffee, and jump into the water. So Larry Woods would meet me with my teeth chattering and my hair plastered to my head, I thought humorously, trying to tell myself I wasn't actually concerned about how I looked when I met him. Yet I remembered with rare clarity the way Larry Woods looked as he dozed on the chaise yesterday.

I changed into a swimsuit, brought a cover-up from the closet to slip into for breakfast, rummaged for thonged sandals for my feet. I was startled at my eagerness to be down at the pool and to meet Larry Woods.

Reluctantly I left my door unlocked, the key hidden away in a drawer. Jeanne would be in soon to do the room. Later, I promised myself, I'd lock the door again. Nobody would have any reason for trying the door—except someone who was up to no good. This morning I felt absurdly childish about this precaution, which yesterday had pleased me.

At the head of the stairs, my mind preoccupied, I almost collided headlong with Jeanne, ascending with a breakfast tray. Grandmère's, I realized.

"Pardonez-moi, Mademoiselle!" Jeanne was wide-eyed with apology as she recovered from the near-dumping of the tray in her hands. "You did not ring. Did you wish breakfast brought to your room?" Her smile vivacious, appealing.

"Thank you, no." I wasn't aware that I might have rung for breakfast. "I'll go downstairs."

Again, feeling faintly ill at ease in this elegant chateau, I walked back towards the family dining room. Lisette's voice drifted towards me, reporting a recent comic encounter with her piano teacher.

I hesitated at the dining room door, finding a poignant delight in the tableau of Dad trying to eat breakfast with Lisette hanging at his shoulder. But I knew he thoroughly enjoyed this display of affection.

And then my eyes moved about the table and clashed with Pat's. Such anger on her face! And suddenly I understood. For a little while she'd played a game where she was the mistress of Chateau Laval, watching her husband and child in a demonstrative moment. But I destroyed this precious interlude for her.

There was no anger in me for Pat Fraser. Only compassion. I wished I'd stayed in my room for another half hour.

"Andrea, are you wearing a swimsuit under that?" Lisette demanded.

"Yes." I forced myself to include Pat in the glance I swept about the table. "I thought I'd have coffee and then go for a swim with you."

"Sit down, Andrea," Dad coaxed. "Claudine's brioches are delicious. You must try them." He was pushing a basket of still-hot brioches, nestled beneath a napkin, towards me as I sat at the table. "I'll ring for another cup and more coffee."

"I'll tell Henri," Pat said quickly, pushing back her chair. "I always take a second cup of coffee into the office with me," she said with strained politeness.

Lisette was impatient now for the two of us to be out at the pool.

"I think I hear Larry out there." She squinted in concentration.

"If he's there, Larry will wait," Dad said calmly. "Please allow Andrea to have her breakfast."

Henri arrived with a cup and saucer for me and a pot of fresh coffee. Dad talked with anticipation about our brief trip into Copenhagen, a city he loved. Lisette went to the window to see if Larry was at the pool.

"Maybe he's coming up the walk. I'll go see," Lisette decided. "May I, Father?"

"All right, Lisette, you are excused." He waited until she was out of hearing range to continue. "Lisette is so delighted that you are here, Andrea. It is lonely, being an only child. And your grandmother makes such demands of her." He sighed, his eyes unhappy. "Perhaps she will be happy at the English school."

Twenty minutes later, fortified with Claudine's marvelous brioches and hot coffee, I allowed Lisette, now back in the dining room, to drag me to the pool. Dad reminded us that all doors must be kept locked. Lisette was solemn, nodding her understanding. Everybody had been briefed.

I felt uncomfortable at being responsible for these security measures. I still clung to the belief that someone within the chateau was responsible for the threats to me, yet I knew I must accept Dad's interpretation of what had happened.

Dad remained at the table. Lisette and I went out through the kitchen door so that Claudine might lock this behind us. She did this, I thought, with unnecessary force.

The morning air was deliciously crisp. Too cool for swimming, I decided, tugging my robe more tightly about me. Lisette seemed not to mind the chill in the air. She pulled off her robe, tossed it into a chaise, gazing about with disappointment.

"Larry is not here yet."

I spyed a figure coming up the driveway.

"There he is, Lisette."

It was ridiculous, but without his opening his mouth to say a word, I'd decided I liked Larry Woods. I liked the friendly curiosity in his hazel eyes. His ready smile. The zest for life that emanated from him.

"The water's cold," Lisette jibed ebulliently. "I'll bet you won't jump right in."

"I'll bet you I will," he said, shedding his own robe. "Hi, I'm Larry Woods," he introduced himself. "You're the wonderful new sister, Andrea Laval."

"I guess the whole village knows there's a new sister," I laughed. But I relished his obvious approval.

"Come on," Lisette urged with a pixie grin. "I dare you to jump in."

With a wink for me, Larry walked to the edge of the pool, jumped in, came up pantomining coldness. Lisette joined him, squealing with the first shock of the night-cold water. I hovered at the edge, not yet brave enough to take the leap.

"Come on in," Lisette coaxed. "Andrea, please." She was so anxious to bring Larry and me together.

Gritting my teeth, I abandoned my cover-up, hesitated, then jumped in, vocally reproachful about the first shock of the icy water. But I remained and enjoyed the water game Larry instituted for the three of us.

I understood why Lisette made no complaint about the summer tutoring. She enjoyed the time with Larry, who no doubt made learning fun. He must be a dedicated teacher, I decided. The kind who really cared.

None of us remained in the water long. We stretched on chaises enjoying the warmth of the sun.

"How do you like Switzerland?" Larry's eyes were serious. He must know the full story of my being here. The drama of my finding my other family.

"What I've seen of it is marvelous." It was a recurrent miracle to me to sit here and gaze out at the panorama spread before us.

"You'll have to see more," Larry said firmly. "What about a drive this afternoon? Phillipe and I share a beat-up Fiat, but it still makes these hills."

"I'd love it." I accepted with amusement at Lisette's gleeful eavesdropping.

"Around four?"

"Great." I nodded enthusiastically. A dozen questions raced through my head. "How long have you been here?"

"I landed in Europe a year ago last month," Larry said leisurely. "I went to England for ten days, then spent a week in Copenhagen before I flew here. I came to Europe," he said seriously, "because I wanted to see how the rest of the world lives. Most weekends Phillipe and I fly somewhere—or if it's close enough we drive." He grinned ruefully. "Terrible strain on the budget, but our rent is practically nothing and we cut corners stringently to allow for the traveling. For the summer months we've grounded ourselves." He shuddered expressively. "Those hordes of tourists!"

"Is Phillipe Swiss or American?"

"French," Larry said with a chuckle. "He's a psychologist at the school. He's also working on a book. The job here ties in with his research. We'll both cut out after the next school year. Phillipe wants to see the States. I want to go back and move into the political scene. That's where the action's going to be these next years."

"I'm going to Copenhagen with Dad on Thursday," I said after a moment, self-conscious before the intensity of Larry's gaze. "We're just staying overnight."

"Copenhagen is a fascinating city," Larry said reminiscently. "You won't be there long enough see much more than the Stroget and Tivoli Gardens. There's a boat tour to Malmo—"

"In Sweden," I said with pleased recognition. "I met someone at a UN party in New York who lived there." The Svedborg's party, the night I met Dad.

"Phillipe and I took the tour." Larry leaned over to pick up a small ball that lay beside the chaise and threw it. Heidi came galloping towards us, big as a pony, intent on retrieving the ball. "You take a bus at City Hall Square in Copenhagen, ride right onto the ferry boat that takes you to Sweden. You're on the Baltic Sea," he recalled. "In an hour you're in Sweden, where you visit Malmo and Lund." Suddenly he chuckled. "On another bus tour, driving outside of Copenhagen, into the country past quaint thatched cottages, we passed one with a roof on which grass grew. I never expect to see the likes of that again!"

"Excuse me, I have to go mow my roof," I laughed.

Heidi came charging towards us now, dumped the ball in my lap.

"I've been replaced," Larry grinned. "You're the Number One Guest to Heidi now."

"I love her madly." I scratched her behind the ears for a moment before I tossed the ball again.

"Basically," Larry said fondly, "Heidi is Lisette's dog. She can't wait for Lisette to come from school on holidays." He reached out to tickle Lisette, who squealed with pleasure at this show of attention.

Five minutes later, with a glint of regret in his eyes, Larry announced it was time for Lisette and him to go inside to tackle English grammar.

"Heidi will keep you company," Larry said. "Remember, I'm picking you up at four."

* * *

Ten minutes before Larry was scheduled to arrive, I stood on the terrace before the chateau astonished that I was so eager to see him again. From the terrace I spied Larry emerging from the small pink house on the tier below. He climbed behind the wheel of the Fiat that sat before the house, then headed for the road.

I hurried down the steps as the Fiat approached. There was a lilt in my voice as I greeted Larry. The ugliness of the slashed dress, the pasted-up message of warning was tucked away in a corner of my mind now. I was on a fantastic holiday, going out with someone I found particularly interesting. It was going to be a great afternoon.

"Feel like driving into Geneva?" Larry asked when I was settled on the seat beside him. I turned to him with astonishment. "It's only about a twenty-five minute drive."

"It sounds wonderful!" My second afternoon at the chateau, and here I was en route to Geneva.

We drove at the subdued rate necessitated by the narrow, curving road towards Bougy Villars, hearing the sound of martial music as we neared the village.

"It's Swiss Independence Day," Larry reminded me, and

I noticed the flags on display before the modest houses. "That'll be the local band."

In the village, in the middle of the street the uniformed band played exuberantly for the assemblage. People courteously moved in order that we might pass through. A pair of little girls in native costumes of an earlier Switzerland waved to us.

"There's Pat and Lisette!" I leaned forward for a better view, waved towards them enthusiastically.

Pat saw me, waved back with reserve. Lisette didn't see me until Pat nudged her. She had found a friend. A boy about her age, with an engaging black mutt. While Lisette and the tail-wagging dog watched, the boy surreptitiously shot off a small firecracker.

"Later tonight there'll be fireworks," Larry told me. "They put on quite a show. This is the Swiss equivalent to our Fourth of July."

We drove through Bougy Villars, began the roundabout descent to the auto-route. Larry talked earnestly about his work at the school, the differences between schools in Switzerland and in America, where he had taught in a ghetto area.

"I grew up in suburban Connecticut," he said with a tone of self-mockery, "then I went to a big city college and learned about the rest of the world. It was a shock. I asked for an assignment in a ghetto school to see what it was like. Then I decided to come to Europe, to see what it was like here. We live in such an opulent oasis in America—or certainly some people do."

"I learned a little about that at the UN," I admitted somberly. "Mr. Svedborg works with the developing nations, and I type up his reports."

"We're shocked at the tax rate in the European countries," Larry pursued. "I think it's about forty percent in England, a little over forty in Denmark and Sweden. But all over Europe—even in Canada—people live without the constant fear of financial disaster from a family illness."

I leaned back, listening to Larry, forgetting the ugliness at the chateau. An exquisitely disturbing belief began taking root in me that Larry Woods was to loom importantly in my life.

"I'll give you a capsule version of the Geneva bus tour,"

Larry promised as we approached the city. "We won't park until we're ready to go in for dinner. Parking is a dirty word in Geneva." His eyes rested on me with amusement because my eyes widened in astonishment at the mention of dinner. I'd thought we were merely out for an afternoon's ride. "You're not worried about reporting in at the chateau for dinner?" he asked.

"I didn't say I wouldn't be home for dinner," I explained hesitantly.

"So we'll find a phone and you'll call your father," he said casually. And it felt so good to hear Larry refer to Dad as my father, with no snide undertones.

"Of course," I agreed softly. Call my father. Not my grandmother, who, thus far, refused to recognize me. Inwardly she refused. Somehow, I was relieved to be away from the chateau for these hours. Not until now did I realize how painfully tense I was.

We drove past the old railroad station, with its crowded terrace café. What a contrast to the strikingly modern airport! We traveled slowly through the tourist-thronged streets with their colorful sidewalk cafés, and Larry pointed out landmarks here and there. The preponderance of jewelry stores was awesome. Then the poignantly beautiful view of lake and mountains lay before us, the Jet d'Eau zipping high into the air.

"The fountain was created in 1886 by an engineer in charge of the local water supply. Today 110 gallons are pumped every second, at a speed of 125 miles an hour," Larry reported with respect. "We know spring is here when the flowers begin to bloom along the quais and the Jet d'Eau is in operation."

We drove across the bridge, just beyond the point where the Rhone leaves Lake Geneva.

"There's the Ile d'Rousseau," Larry pointed to a tiny island as we drove. "There's a statue of Rousseau and probably the smallest merry-go-ground you've ever seen. And of course benches for people who want to admire the scenery."

We saw the historic flower clock, the Russian Church with its nine spires covered with gold leaf. We passed the local prison, euphemistically called the Refuge of St. Anthony. Then Larry decided to drive into the Old City, past

56

the chapel that was once Calvin's. We saw in the distance the three spires of St. Peter's.

I was disappointed at first sight of the United Nations Palace because I have a running love affair with our UN buildings in New York. Though, I acknowledged, the World Health Building was dramatically modern.

"There's a conference hall farther along here," Larry recounted, "that was built without windows so that the delegates will concentrate on work rather than on the views."

Now Larry decided it was time to locate a parking spot.

"It's always a problem in Geneva," he warned grimly. "Worse than in New York. But there's one place I know where they may be able to take us in."

We were in luck. There was room for the Fiat. With the car parked, we headed back for the lakeshore, to walk through the dramatic formal gardens, laid out with geometric precision and an eye for color, to the restaurant where Larry had decided we'd have dinner.

"Other nights I'll take you to some charming, budget places, but tonight we'll dine in style," he teased. "At the Perle du Lac, right on the lake."

The walk was longer than I'd expected—longer than Larry remembered, but we didn't mind. Not with that incredible view, at our right. I listened to the medly of languages spoken on all sides. Inspected the variety of costumes. The casual attire of the tourists, the exotic dress of the Asians, the dungareed, sneakered look of the college hordes. A few women in high fashion outfits, usually Europeans.

"Glad you came to Switzerland?" Larry asked when we were seated at a table on the restaurant terrace—facing, as Larry had promised, directly on the lake. Only a few tables were occupied this early. Most diners preferred a fashionably late hour, when the lights of Geneva would be on display. But we would dawdle over dinner, to remain until dark. I'd stopped to phone the chateau. There was no need to rush. "Or do you wish you'd gone to Scandinavia with your roommates?" Larry's eyes teased me.

"Nothing could make me regret coming to the chateau," I said impetuously. "Not even that insane note—" I stopped dead. Hearing those careless words echoing in the sudden silence. Aware of the instant curiosity—or was it something else?—in Larry's eyes.

"What insane note?" His tone was casual. Not so his eyes.

"I shouldn't have mentioned it." What was the matter with me? Yet there was this compulsion in me to share this with Larry. "There was this note—a paste-up of letters from a newspaper. I found it shoved under my bedroom door. It said—" I took a deep breath. "It said, 'American, go home. Or die.' " I forced a smile. "Isn't that taking anti-Americanism too far?"

"What did your father say?" Larry's voice was serious.

"He was furious. He figures some stranger wandered into the chateau, and shoved the note under my door."

"I don't buy that," Larry said quickly, and my heart pounded. "How would a stranger know which room was yours? Andrea, I don't like this."

"Dad's reporting it to the police. In Aubonne and in Bougy Villars." I hesitated, fighting to sound calm. "He said there are a lot of tourists in the area this time of the year."

"No tourist sneaked into the chateau and put that note under your door," Larry insisted grimly. "What else is your father doing about this?"

"The doors are being kept locked around the clock," I reported. "At night all the shutters on the lower floor are being locked. It would take some doing to scale the walls to the second floor balconies that lead to the bedrooms."

"Andrea, can't you make him understand this is not the work of somebody living outside the chateau?" Larry leaned forward intently. "Someone who lives in the chateau is responsible. And I find that disturbing."

"Dad couldn't ever accept that theory, Larry." I shook my head with conviction. "Both Henri and Claudine have been with the family for many years. Pat, too. The only newcomer among the staff is Jeanne, and I know she couldn't have done it."

"Andrea, everybody is suspect," Larry said quietly. He hesitated. "It might be wiser for you to move into the family apartment in the city until your father can come up with some answers. He has a beautiful apartment with marvelous views. I was there once for dinner with Phillipe."

"Leave the chateau because of that note?" I tried to laugh this off while fighting an urge to confide in Larry about the slashed dress. I knew he would consider it with the same seriousness as I. But suddenly everything was jumping out of focus. Alarm churned in me. The pat words I'd framed in my mind about the absurdity of all this sounded hollow. "No, I'll be all right," I insisted. "Some crackpot is taking pleasure in trying to frighten me away. Henri hates all Americans," I added.

"I've heard." Larry nodded.

"I know it's unfair to try to pin this on someone without proof—but he looks at me with such hatred." Claudine looked at me with hatred. And Pat Fraser. Even my own grandmother was hostile beneath a veneer of politeness.

"Did you discuss this in depth with your father?" Larry probed.

"No. I've—I've tried to laugh it off." If I allowed myself to take that threat seriously, I'd pack up and board the next 747 bound for New York.

What would Larry say if I told him about the slashed dress? *No.* Don't tell him. He might go to Dad. He's genuinely upset, knowing just about the note.

The waiter came over with the menus. We made an effort to concentrate on ordering. Additional diners were settling themselves at tables about us. There was a festive air. It was a holiday evening.

Soon the lights would begin to glow in the dusk. I could envision the splendor of the view. But in this fairy-tale setting I sat wrapped in apprehension.

Chapter Six

We took a taxi from the Perle du Lac to where the Fiat was parked, and during the ride my eyes remained fastened to the passing sights knowing that the spectacle of Geneva at night would forever remain with me. In the Fiat we headed for the auto-route. On the way Larry pointed out the elegant building where the family apartment was located.

I was astonished by the heavy traffic until I realized that, for many, this was the conclusion of a four-day holiday weekend. While there was none of the bumper-to-bumper traffic I recalled on such weekends back home, the line-up of cars was impressive.

"Cool?" Larry asked.

"A little," I admitted, and he promptly raised the window on his side. Mine was already shut.

Larry experimented with the radio until he found music that pleased him.

"When I first came to Geneva, I tried renting a car," he said. "They didn't have radios. I was indignant. Luckily I met Phillipe soon after school opened. I got out of my hotel, moved into the house with him, and we bought this bug."

"Larry, what's the real story in Switzerland on the American question? *Do* they hate us?" In my mind I was hoping to write off the ugly happenings at the chateau on this impersonal basis, while instinct shouted "No!"

Larry was silent for a moment. Searching for words. Guessing what was behind my question.

"A lot of Swiss are upset about the heavy tourist inflow every summer," Larry acknowledged. "They forget its importance to the Swiss economy. Not just Americans. Europeans and Asians as well. Walking through the streets, you can understand why. Of course, a lot of Genevans leave the city during July and August. It's not the most comfortable of cities in the summer, with air-conditioning so rare."

"I read somewhere that there's some effort now on the part of the government to keep jobs open for the Swiss. But that didn't stop you," I teased.

"I got through," Larry admitted with a grin. "But it's true that they don't encourage Americans to move here. And if you've ever tried to look for a house near Geneva, you'd understand why fewer and fewer Americans are settling over here. Living accommodations, except for summer tourist rentals, are just non-existent, unless you're willing to lay out a hundred thousand—dollars, not francs—for a condominium apartment. Complete with roof-top swimming pools in some cases. The expatriates are now heading for Istanbul where you can rent a villa for seventy dollars a month and hire a full-time maid for thirty."

We were moving steadily along the auto-route despite the traffic. I didn't care how long it would take us to reach the chateau. It was cozy with the windows up in the car, with the music playing softly into the background, with Larry beside me. I felt as though I'd known him forever, rather than just a day.

"You'll have to give me the phone number at the chateau," Larry told me. "It's unlisted."

I gazed at him in amazement.

"Larry, you gave me the number to call before when I'd phoned to say I wouldn't be home for dinner."

"That's the office line," Larry explained with a smile. "Your father gave that number to Phillipe a long time ago. But there's another number for the other phones in the house. I wouldn't want to have to disturb your father every time I called you."

"I'll make a note of it and tell you," I promised. I tingled with the implication that Larry expected to see much of me.

At Rolle we left the auto-route to begin the circuitous drive up the side of the mountain through the dark vineyards. Off the auto-route the roads were deserted. We circled higher and higher without encountering one car. Just before the turn-off into Bougy Villars we slowed to a crawl to watch a burst of fireworks below.

"The fireworks at the Tivoli Gardens in Copenhagen are spectacular," Larry told me. "They have them on one midweek night and on Saturdays during the season. I arrived in Copenhagen from London on a Saturday. That night I watched the fireworks from my room. A six-flight walk-up," he reminisced. "But it was clean and cheap."

"I'm intrigued by the closeness of everything," I said with a burst of enthusiasm. "An hour or two by plane and you're in most of the capitals of Europe."

"That's why I took the teaching job here," Larry pointed out. "So I could have my fabulous weekends." His eyes left the wheel to rest fleetingly on me. "You wouldn't consider staying on indefinitely in Switzerland? Like for maybe a year?" he pursued with a grin.

"Larry, I have a job back in New York," I protested. But my heart thumped at the implication in his eyes. "Dad's hinted that he'd like to see me stay on," I conceded. Plenty of room for me in the apartment, he'd said with emphasis. "Of course, somebody at the chateau would be terribly unhappy if I stayed on. All this fuss over my being here just for the month of August—"

"Stop off at the house and have coffee with Phillipe and me," Larry urged. "He writes in the evenings, but by this time he will have stopped. I'd like to have his reaction to that note. Phillipe dissects everything with scientific thoroughness. I'm inclined to be hotheaded."

"I'll stop for coffee," I stipulated. "But please, Larry, don't mention the note." I felt oddly disloyal to Dad in discussing this even with Larry.

We drove through Bougy Villars, whose houses were dark for the night.

As we turned into the driveway before the pink house, we could hear a fine recording of Dvorák's *New World Symphony*.

"Phillipe is a classical music buff," Larry explained as we pulled up before the door of the house.

Here the shutters were closed tight on the lower floor, except at the one lighted room.

"It looks as though everybody around here is boarded up against a storm, doesn't it?" Larry chuckled. "I don't know whether it's against intruders or the insects from the vineyards. Nobody has screens here, you may have noticed. Except for you fancy people up at the chateau," he jibed. "Phillipe and I invested in one custom-made screen for our living room. We like to sit there and watch the storms over the lake and the mountains. Wow, it's a show!"

We left the car, walked to the door. Larry pulled it wide and I walked inside. Half a flight of stone stairs led up to the foyer.

Someone was in the tiny kitchen directly ahead, at the range. He turned around, momentarily startled to discover Larry was not alone.

"Hello." A warm, casual smile. "I'm Phillipe." He was not quite as tall as Larry. Five or six years older, I judged, with dark hair, dark eyes. Beautiful hands, I noticed subconsciously. A man who knew where he was going.

"Andrea Laval," I said lightly before Larry could introduce us.

"You resemble Lisette," Phillipe decided, gazing appraisingly at me. "But without her vein of granite."

"You don't like Lisette," I accused him disturbed by his remark.

"I think her grandmother and the servants are raising her in a hothouse atmosphere that's going to ruin her," Phillipe said flatly, and I guessed that Larry and he had discussed this fully.

"Phillipe is writing a book on child psychology," Larry said good-humoredly. "No child gets within sight of him without being analyzed. When will the coffee be ready, Phillipe?"

"Four or five minutes. Turn off the record player, would you, Larry? It's distracting when we want to talk."

Larry led me into the square, living room with its cathedral ceiling and crossed to switch off the record player. I stood for a moment, admiring the room. The dining area was on the right. There were chairs on two sides of the table and a built-in, L-shaped seat serviced the other two sides. A low bowl of roses sat on the table. The floor was covered with deep-red tile.

At our left was a brick fireplace flanked on both sides by

tall well-stacked bookcases. A bank of windows opened wide to face the lake and the mountains. French doors opened onto a patio where I could see a table and chairs. What a pleasant place for a meal, I thought.

"Come sit over here," Larry invited, prodding me towards several comfortable chairs before the window, with a window seat comfortably available as a footrest. "We don't live in a chateau, but we have a view worthy of one."

Phillipe joined us with the coffee tray. A plate of pastries, bought from the shop in Aubonne, I guessed, graced the tray.

"I was fascinated by the story of your meeting with your father," Phillipe said with candor. "No drama concocted by the storytellers can surpass those of real life. How is Lisette taking it?"

"What do you mean?" I was bewildered.

"Is she upset at being removed from the spotlight?"

"Lisette is wonderful," I said with reproach. "She's done everything possible to make me feel welcome." I hesitated. "But Henri and Claudine are not friendly. Nor is my grandmother."

"Madame Laval must have been quite upset," Phillipe conceded with unexpected compassion. "To be presented with a grown-up granddaughter, right out of the blue."

"I doubt that she believes I *am* her granddaughter," I said, suddenly uneasy. *Why had I said that?*

"You can prove it, Andrea?" Larry was startled. He hadn't believed that there was any question about my identity.

"I wrote away for my birth certificate. It must show my father's name." *Why was I talking so much?*

"How did your mother rationalize keeping your father a secret all these years?" Phillipe pressed, and I could see myself already becoming a case history in the book he was writing.

"Mother was very young when I was born," I stammered defensively. "She was terrified at the prospect of living in Europe. She—she ran off with me." My back was up at this attack on my mother, even while I still churned with anger at what she had done to Dad and me. *But it wasn't Phillipe's business.*

64

"Andrea—" Phillipe leaned forward. His eyes were hypnotic. "Andrea, if you are the bright girl I think you are, you will get out of that chateau tomorrow. Stay in the Laval apartment in Geneva if you will—but get out of the chateau."

My eyes swung accusingly to Larry. He'd told Phillipe about the note!

"I said nothing to Phillipe about the note," Larry assured me earnestly. "I swear it, Andrea."

"What note?" Phillipe asked quietly. An air of authority in his voice commanded me to tell him. While I was defensive before Phillipe, deep in the recesses of my mind I understood he was genuinely concerned for me. "What is this all about, Andrea?"

"A note was stuck under my bedroom door yesterday." I struggled to sound matter-of-fact. Why was Phillipe so insistent that I leave? What did he know that he was telling neither Larry nor me? Or what did he suspect? "A fairly routine note," I continued with an air of defiance. " 'American, go home.' " I took a deep breath. " ' Or die'. Someone with a flair for the melodramatic." I forced a seemingly amused smile, fooling neither Phillipe nor Larry. "Dad is convinced some tourist passing through the area is responsible."

"There is in the chateau such an atmosphere of tragedy. Of more than that," Phillipe emphasized. "Of watchfulness. As though in anticipation of more disaster. I cannot figure out yet why I say this, Andrea," he acknowledged with honesty, "but I feel this is a bad place for you to be."

"You working on instinct?" Larry derided gently. "The man of science?"

"The atmosphere of tragedy isn't difficult to comprehend," I stated. "Dad's second wife and my brother died in a boating accident six years ago."

"We know," Phillipe said gently. "Monsieur Laval has told us about this. That is the kind of tragedy that remains forever with those whom it has touched. That is why, of course, Lisette is being raised under such tensions. This business of changing from school to school each year. Her grandmother's demands. It is devastating for the child. Andrea—" He leaned urgently towards me. "Talk to your father about this. Make him understand that Lisette desperately needs roots. She must remain in one school, the pressures must be relaxed. All these activities—the music, the painting, the dancing—it is too much. Every hour must not be structured during the school year. She must have some freedom."

Yet again, I sensed in Phillipe a dislike for Lisette. His training forced him to make these assessments. He was being honest as a child psychologist. But he didn't like my sister; and this would keep a wall between us. A shame, because I could have so easily liked Larry's house-sharer.

"I'll talk to Dad," I promised. "But I doubt that it'll help. Grandmère rules when it comes to Lisette."

"Andrea, try these pastries," Larry coaxed, and I knew he was determined to rechannel the conversation into less disturbing areas. "They're fabulous."

Half an hour later Larry drove me up to the chateau. We'd swim again in the morning, we'd decided, before Lisette's tutoring. In the afternoon he would drive me to Ferney, where Voltaire spent the last years of his life. I'd told Larry how everything about Voltaire intrigued me.

"There's a Voltaire Café in Ferney," Larry teased. "We'll go there for coffee and atmosphere."

"It's been a marvelous day," I said while we waited for someone to open the door.

"I'm glad you came to Switzerland," Larry told me, his eyes saying much more. Oh, this was too fast, my mind warned. Too fast! But my heart rejoiced.

"I'm glad, too, Larry," I said softly.

Henri opened the door with an air of barely concealed irritation. Guiltily I realized that Claudine and he were up quite early. Probably by this hour they were normally asleep. But tonight Henri knew I was out for the evening. He remained up to admit me.

"Bon soir, Mademoiselle, Monsieur," he said formally, holding the door wide.

"Bon soir, Henri." I waved farewell to Larry.

I crossed quickly to the stairs, walked up to my room. Glancing surreptiously up and down the hall when I reached my door, I scrounged around in my purse for the key. A key, my mind taunted, which any ill-wisher could so easily duplicate.

Inside my room I locked the door, crossed to the windows to draw the drapies tight. At the balcony I paused, intrigued by the brilliant display of fireworks farther down on the mountainside. The last audacious burst, I surmised. The colors flashed dramatically against the night sky.

I started at the sound of a light knock on the door and moved quickly to answer it. My mind was alert to the necessity for turning that key in the door before I touched the doorknob. I didn't want anyone—except the person who had invaded my room yesterday—to know this door was locked. Not even Dad, I thought uneasily.

"Heidi, what are you doing out there?" Dad's voice reprimanded the animal in the hall. "Come, come back to Lisette."

With relief, I quickly turned the key, opened the door, pulled it wide. I slipped the key out of sight.

"Dad?" I leaned forward with a smile. He was opening the door to Lisette's room, prodding Heidi inside with a gentle pat on the rump.

"Andrea." He walked towards me with a glow of pleasure. "I thought I heard you come in. Did you have a good day?"

"Lovely," I said frankly.

"I came to tell you to look out your window at the fireworks," Dad explained. "They're spectacular.

"I know," I said enthusiastically. "I was just—"

I stopped with a shock. A sharp report, like a small explosion, had rocked my room. His face etched with alarm, Dad pulled me further into the corridor.

"Stay here," he ordered.

"Dad, be careful!" My inclination was to drag him back into the safety of the hall, but he was already stalking into my room.

I disregarded his command and followed at his heels. My eyes were wide as I surveyed the floor of my room. Not immediately assimilating what had happened, I stared uncomprehendingly at the bits of cardboard, the fragment of rope that littered the floor. A jagged hole was burnt in the gold carpeting just inside the French doors where I had been standing a moment ago.

"Firecrackers!" Dad's voice was choked with rage. "You

could have been badly hurt. What kind of idiot would do a thing like this?" He crossed swiftly to the balcony, leaned out to inspect the area with frustration. "Whoever did this stood below and tossed the handful of firecrackers, tied together with the rope, into the room. It didn't take much skill." *My* room, my mind registered. Deliberately my room. "Perhaps we should keep Heidi outdoors nights. But she is spoiled." He frowned in concentration. "We must do something to prevent a recurrence of this."

"Should I check on Lisette?" I asked. "Do you suppose she was frightened?"

Dad's face brightened. He adored Lisette.

"When Lisette sleeps, nothing disturbs her. She feels so secure with Heidi in her room."

"Armand!" Grandmère's voice called anxiously in the corridor. "What's happening?"

"It is all right, Maman," Dad called back soothingly. "Just a ridiculous prank."

"I tried your room and there was no response," Grandmère said in my doorway. "And then I went to Lisette's room. Armand, you are allowing her to have the dog in her room again."

"Maman, she feels happy with Heidi," Dad said placatingly.

Now Grandmère's eyes focused on the carpet.

"Armand, what's happened?" Her voice faintly strident with shock. "I heard that awful noise—"

"Some prankster tossed a bundle of firecrackers into Andrea's room," Dad explained, his eyes disturbed. "She could have been badly hurt."

"I'll call Henri to prepare another room for the night." Grandmère was pale, but she refused to lose her calm. "You can't sleep in here tonight, Andrea."

"It's all right," I said quickly. Perversely I wanted to stay here. I was reluctant to gamble on yet another room. "There's only the hole in the carpeting."

"But that awful aroma." Grandmère crinkled her nose in distaste. "How can you sleep with it in the room?"

"It won't bother me," I insisted with a casualness I didn't feel. My instinct, once I was alone, would be to pick up the phone and call Larry. But that would be slightly hysterical, wouldn't it? I wasn't hurt. It could wait until tomorrow.

68

But if Dad hadn't knocked at just that moment, pulling me away from the French doors, I could have been badly burned or blinded.

That was the intent of whoever tossed those firecrackers into my room.

Chapter Seven

Dad walked Grandmère to her room. I closed my door, carefully locked it, crossed to the balcony, shuddering as I gazed out into the darkness of the night. The sky was overcast and ominous now.

I pulled the French doors tight, locked them. Dad was convinced this had been a prank perpetrated by someone too stupid to realize he could cause serious injury. Even death. But the note had said, "go home or die". The slashes in my dress had been terrifyingly eloquent.

I locked the casement windows, though I would have enjoyed the fresh mountain air as I slept. Moving about the room preparing for bed, I made a conscious effort not to look at the dark hole in the carpet.

Outside, a storm was brewing. I stiffened at the sound of thunder. I was feeling frighteningly alone, locked in my room this way. I remembered how Larry had said that Phillipe and he enjoyed watching the storms from their windows that faced the lake.

Ready for bed, I still hesitated at climbing beneath the cozy wool blanket. I stood self-consciously at the side of the bed for what seemed like minutes before I capitulated. But still I felt childishly reluctant to switch off the lamps. Oh, this was absurd! *Turn off the lamps.*

I lay stiffly alert in the darkness listening to the claps of thunder, the sound of a car on the road below, trying to out-race the storm, a shutter banging somewhere downstairs, until someone fastened it tight.

I could hear no rain. Not yet. Only the Wagnerian rolls of thunder that seemed to shake the chateau. Compulsively I thrust aside the blanket, left the bed to walk barefoot to the balcony doors, reaching for my robe that lay on a chair at the balcony before I pulled the door open.

Standing at the open door, I gazed out at the drama of the impending storm. Such magnificence! Lightning zig-zagged across the sky, illuminating the churning dark waters of the lake and providing an eerie display of the awesome mountains. On the opposite shore I could see the red lights, blinking warnings to any boat that might be out at this hour, calling them in because of the threatening weather.

Traffic on the auto-route was sparse. The small houses on the mountainside were dark now except for two rooms lighted in Larry's and Phillipe's house. Not a car on the country roads. And in the midst of this spectacular beauty, such ugliness lurked in the shadows.

Someone from the chateau could have gone out to throw those firecrackers into my room, and returned without being noticed. It was late, I reasoned. Bedtime already. But how was it only Dad and Grandmère had shown up at the sound of the explosion? *How could the others not have heard?*

Again, I thought wistfully of reaching for the phone to call Larry. Caution stopped me. How could I know who might not pick up a phone somewhere in the chateau, listen to what I would say to Larry? Tomorrow I would tell Larry about this new happening.

Suddenly the rain came down with stunning force. I re-treated. Another minute here and I would be soaked to the skin. With the door shut, and locked, the draperies drawn tight, I returned to the bed, pulled the blanket snugly about my shoulders, willing myself to sleep.

* * *

I came awake slowly, hearing sounds in the chateau, voices outdoors. The storm was over. I turned over to face the clock on my night table. Almost nine. Larry would be over at ten for a swim.

Instantly I was wide awake remembering last night. I was impatient for Larry to arrive so I could confide in him.

71

What would he say about this newest attempt on my life? Yes, I told myself resolutely. *This* was an attempt on my life. The dress, the note, were attempts to frighten me away.

I reached for the robe that I'd left across the foot of my bed last night. Pulling its warmth about me, I crossed to the balcony, opened the doors to the splendor of the morning. The sky was a brilliant blue, a dramatic contrast to last night's storm. No haze this morning. The mountains—even Mont Blanc—were on glorious display. The lake was beautifully calm and blue.

"Good morning!" Dad's voice brought my gaze down to the terrace. He sat at a table with Pat, having breakfast while they discussed business, I gathered from the open manila folder before Dad.

"Good morning," I leaned over the railing with a quick smile for both.

"How do you feel?" Pat asked with unexpected solicitude.

"Fine." For a few moments I'd forgotten what hovered over me.

"I think it's dreadful about those firecrackers," Pat said with a look of pain. "I didn't hear a thing. I'd taken a sleeping pill because I had a bad headache."

"I've told Pat to phone a Geneva employment agency about a night watchman for a couple of weeks," Dad said seriously. "We'll have the grounds covered from dusk to sunup."

"That should keep out crackpots," I forced myself to say casually. But I didn't believe this was some outsider. "I'd better get dressed now. See you later."

Feeling melodramatic, I went to the door that led to the hall to remove the key. The door must be unlocked when Jeanne came to do my room. I put the key in the pocket of the terrycloth beach robe I meant to wear downstairs.

While I brushed my hair someone knocked. Jeanne, or perhaps Lisette, I guessed. I went quickly to the door with a smile of welcome for either.

"Bon jour, Mademoiselle." Jeanne greeted me vivaciously. "Monsieur Laval tells me to bring you coffee. You are awake, he said."

"Oh, how nice, Jeanne." I gazed appreciatively at the attractive tray with its small carafe of fragrant coffee, color-ful modern china and napkin-wrapped, still-hot croissants on a plate.

"*Mon Dieu!*" Jeanne was gaping, aghast, at the hole in the carpeting. "Mademoiselle, what happened?"

"Someone threw in a handful of firecrackers," I explained with false nonchalance. "Rather overdoing the Independence Day celebration."

"You were in the room?" She was horrified.

"I'd just gone to the door."

"Mademoiselle, you might have been killed!"

"But I wasn't." I forced a smile. "Wow, that coffee smells delicious."

"Shall I put the tray here for you?" Jeanne indicated a small table near the balcony doors. Her eyes moved compulsively to that burnt segment of the carpet.

"That'll be fine."

Jeanne gazed at me with a disconcerting intensity as she put down the tray.

"Do you like living here, Mademoiselle?"

"Oh, yes, it's beautiful!" How could anyone not be charmed by Switzerland?

"Beautiful, yes," Jeanne said with a bitterness that snapped me to attention. "But it is not enough to look at the mountains and the lake. Do you know, Mademoiselle, I have never been farther from the village than Rolle? Never even to Geneva?"

"But it's only a short drive, Jeanne," I protested in astonishment.

"My parents are farmers. Their life is growing grapes. To them it is enough to have a place to sleep, enough to eat, and the mountains to see. Only for a few years have we had even a radio." Now I recalled the scarcity of TV antennas on neighboring houses. We had television at the chateau. Larry and Phillipe had television. But only a scattering of the familiar antennas showed on most of the houses. "But when school opens again," Jeanne went on with sudden pride, "I am to go away to the university." Her eye glowed. "For two years I worked to save for this."

"Jeanne, that's great!"

"Every summer I see students from all over Europe, from America, driving through the vineyards, and I envy

73

them until I ache. But now my time is coming. I, too, will see other places, other people."

I sat down before the tray, my mind dwelling on Jeanne as I ate. Such bitterness, such frustration in her at being kept here in her tiny village. None of it was visible to me until now. How incredible that, with Geneva only a twenty-five minute drive away, she had never travelled beyond Rolle, a small town barely ten minutes away.

Two croissants and two cups of coffee later I went downstairs. In the library Lisette was practicing scales at the piano. I thought with amusement how our grandmother, who loathed all noise, could steel herself to listen to this. The door to the office suite was shut. Dad was dictating to Pat.

I went outside through the kitchen door so that Claudine could lock it behind me without effort. She gave me a grudging nod for this consideration. I knew she resented this security measure, cynically disbelieving, as I was, of its value.

The outdoor air was cool, crisp. Without relinquishing my robe, I stretched out on a chaise beside the pool, glad for the warmth of the sun. I doubted that any of us would go into the pool today.

I saw the postman bicycle up the driveway. I waved. He nodded and continued up the driveway to make his delivery.

How long would it take for my birth certificate to arrive? And when it arrived, what would I do with it, I mused with wry humor? Frame it, present it to my grandmother? Would I ever break down her wall of resentment against me? Even with positive proof that I was her granddaughter?

The postman left, pausing at the bottom of the driveway to talk to someone. I leaned forward to see who it was. Larry. Now the memory of last night smacked me in the face. I churned to confide in Larry, knowing I would find comfort in sharing my fears with him.

"Hi." I leaned forward to wave to him. My heart thumped.

"No swimming this morning," he said. Nor was he dressed for it. "It must be below sixty even now. Phillipe turned the heat on early this morning for half an hour to take away the chill. He got up at seven o'clock to work."

"Am I a case history?" I asked trying to find the words to tell Larry about last night, without sounding melodramatic.

Larry chuckled.

"Everybody is a potential chapter in Phillipe's book. He's deeply involved, you know. Every problem is a challenge."

"He hates Lisette," I said softly. *Why had I said that?* Tell him about last night. "Why, Larry?"

"Honey, he doesn't hate Lisette," Larry rejected gently. "He thinks she's dreadfully spoiled."

"She's beautiful, exceptionally bright, and talented. Phillipe remembers some of the deprived, disturbed children he's worked with—and he resents her," I challenged. "I don't expect him to admit this."

"Come on," Larry reproached. "Don't you start a vendetta with Phillipe. He thinks you're sensational."

But he didn't like Lisette. He could never convince me otherwise.

"Andrea!" Lisette's light voice drifted towards us. Now I would have to wait to tell Larry. "You didn't tell me you were downstairs."

"I wasn't going to disturb your practicing." Affectionately, I accepted her exuberant hug and returned it.

"Grandmère says I can't go swimming this morning," Lisette said with wistful regret, settling herself on the ground beside me her hand reaching for mine.

"None of us are going," Larry soothed. "The water's suitable only for polar bears."

"Henri is driving Grandmère and me into Geneva this afternoon," Lisette said. "Grandmère says we must shop for clothes for school. Come with us, Andrea," she coaxed. "It'll be fun if you're along."

"Not this time, Lisette," I rejected with an air of apology. "I'm going to Ferney with Larry."

"Oh." Her eyes were dark with disappointment. "I guess it really wouldn't be much fun with Grandmère. She hates going into the city in the summer. Because of all the tourists the shops are so crowded."

"Perhaps you and I could go into Geneva some day. Would you like that, Lisette?" I tried to make this sound enticing. "We could have lunch at that lovely place by the lake. What's its name, Larry?"

75

"Perle du Lac," Larry supplied.

"Did you and Larry have lunch there?" Lisette asked wistfully, her eyes moving from Larry to me.

"We had dinner there. Out on the terrace. The restaurant is right there on the lakeshore."

"Can we really go?" Lisette pressed eagerly. "When? This week?"

"Next week," I compromised. "Tomorrow I'm flying to Copenhagen with Dad."

"Oh." Disappointment in her voice made me feel guilty about this jaunt.

"Let's get on with the grammar, Lisette," Larry said with mock sternness, rising from the chaise and extending a hand to her. "I expect you to do me proud at that fancy new school of yours."

Unhappily I watched Larry and Lisette head for the chateau. I'd have to wait until this afternoon to brief Larry about last night.

I remained on the chaise, appreciating the delicious warmth of the sun and computing the time Larry would remain inside with Lisette. An hour, or a few minutes longer at most, and he'd be out again. I'd wait here for him.

Today I was restless. Pleased that Larry was taking me to Ferney after lunch. Impatient for that time to arrive. Grandmère emerged from the chateau, walked to the rose trellis to cut some choice blossoms to take indoors. She gave no sign that she was aware of my presence a hundred feet away.

My sole surviving grandparent, and I might have been a stranger to her. Her attitude upset Dad, though he pretended unawareness. It upset me, I admitted reluctantly because I wanted to love her. I wanted to have a grandmother. Did she feel I was cheating Lisette by becoming part of Dad's life again? Ridiculous. I too was his child.

My eyes moved compulsively to my watch, willing the time to pass. Then I spied Larry, and sat up with anticipation. But Lisette trailed directly behind, hurrying to catch up with him. Then they were absorbed in discussion. Oh, I liked his compassion for Lisette!

I struggled to mask my disappointment when Lisette settled on a chaise beside me. Again, I must wait to talk privately with Larry—and with delay this seemed increasingly urgent. Simultaneously I was ashamed of wanting Lisette to be elsewhere at this moment. I was going to be here only a month; let me spend as much time as possible with her.

Poor baby, she was so lonely here at the chateau. Why didn't Dad insist on sending her to one of those marvelous Swiss camps, where she could have companionship? At least, let Grandmère make some kind of arrangement to bring a child here from the village to play with Lisette. She'd played with that boy yesterday when Pat had taken her to see the band concert. She'd seemed to be having such fun. I'd talk to Dad about it, I decided resolutely. That much I could do for Lisette.

Larry lingered briefly with us, Lisette and he talking ebulliently about New York, which Lisette adored. Then he consulted his watch.

"I'd better get home. We've got a standing rule. The house must be shipshape before lunch." He swatted Lisette affectionately, then turned to me. "Pick you up right after lunch, Andrea."

Lisette and I sat watching a pair of sailboats racing on the lake, until I decided we must go to our rooms to dress for lunch. I dreaded going into my room. Last night was still starkly clear in my mind. The acrid odor of the firecrackers had not yet dissipated when I'd come down this morning. I cringed, still, at the knowledge that a stranger had invaded my room, touched my belongings. Someone whose identity I didn't even know.

"I'll be downstairs before you," Lisette challenged with an impish smile. "Bet?"

"Bet," I accepted.

We parted at my door, Lisette darting ahead with elfin grace, her face lit up with this small play. I swung my door wide, stopped dead, my heart pounding. Henri was on his knees by the window. Aware of my presence, he turned his head, rose awkwardly to his feet.

"Pardonez-moi, Mademoiselle," he said formally, and pointed towards the floor.

He had cut away the burnt segment of my carpet and replaced it with a perfect circle of fresh carpeting no doubt prudently saved at the time of installation for some such mishap. No, not this kind of mishap, my mind rejected.

"Thank you, Henri." I tried to smile.

Henri left, closing the door behind him with an unnecessary sharpness. I listened to his disappearing footsteps, waiting until he was on the stairs before locking the door. Then I went about the routine of washing up and changing for lunch. Wool slacks and a sweater, I decided, considering the autumnal coolness of the day. Blue, I decided with a glint of anticipation, because this was the most flattering color I could wear. I made a point of not looking at my suitcase as I reached above it to pull down the slacks. I shivered as I visualized the slashed dress hidden in the suitcase. The action known only to me and to the perpetrator.

The business of the dress upset me more than the note or the firecrackers. It was such a glaringly clear message. Why couldn't I bring myself to tell Dad? But I would tell Larry.

Dressed, I left the room. I hesitated at the door. No, I mustn't use the key anymore. I'd feel awful if Dad found out. He'd know how frightened I was. Besides, the key was a farce, I conceded realistically, available to anyone for a franc.

Lisette was already at the table.

"It's a shame there are no children nearby," I said on impulse while Henri moved about the table serving Claudine's gourmet luncheon. "Especially since there's the pool to enjoy."

"Lisette has companions during the school year." Grandmère's voice was sharp.

"Couldn't there be some arrangement to bring a little girl from the village?" I pursued because Lisette's eyes were fastened compellingly to my face.

Grandmère stared at me, detesting me for interfering.

"These children and Lisette have little in common," she said with irritation. "Please do not concern yourself for Lisette. She has her music. She paints. She swims. It is a relaxing summer for her."

"When we leave tomorrow, Andrea," Dad said, "wear something summery but bring along a light coat. The days in Copenhagen are apt to be New York hot, but the evenings—even in midsummer—are cool."

"I can't wait to see Copenhagen." I glowed with anticipation.

"Why can't I go along?" Lisette asked impetuously. "I

could stay with Andrea while you have your business appointment. Couldn't I, Andrea?"

Before I could reply, Grandmère snapped out a blunt rejection of this.

"You will not go to Copenhagen with your father, Lisette. It is not necessary."

"I'll bring you a surprise, Lisette," I promised with a cajoling smile. "All right?"

"What kind of a surprise?" She was reluctant to abandon the prospect of sharing our trip.

"But it won't be a surprise if I tell you," I teased.

Inadvertently my eyes clashed with my grandmother's. And in that instant I realized that Grandmère resented Lisette's affection for me. It was a chilling assessment.

"I will be driving into Geneva with you this afternoon, Lisette." Dad was anxious to coax her into her usual vivacity. "And Henri will stop by the office with Grandmère and you to pick me up when you have finished your shopping. We will stop somewhere for an ice if Henri can manage to park."

Lisette glowed. How little it took to please her, I thought tenderly. I must buy her something special in Copenhagen, feeling rich because my vacation was costing me nothing. Dad had even insisted on paying my air fare.

After lunch the others returned to their rooms for a rest, as was the habit at the chateau. I went upstairs to my room only to collect my purse and passport.

"I'm going to Ferney with Larry," I told Dad at my door when he lingered to remind me I would need my passport tomorrow. "I'm so excited."

"A true Laval," he said with a surge of satisfaction. "Maman, did you hear? Andrea is making the pilgrimage to Ferney."

But my grandmother, twenty feet beyond us, approaching her own room, preferred not to hear.

In my room I dug into a drawer for my purse remembering, for a painful second, the disorder here the day of the intrusion. *No, don't think about that.* What about a cardigan? Yes, take it along. There may be an even sharper drop in the temperature. And Larry and I will be gone all afternoon.

Why do I feel this oppressiveness? It's broad daylight.

What can possibly happen to me now? What makes me so sure something else is going to happen? Because, I thought, a pattern was forming. The dress, the note, the firecrackers. What next?

Go on downstairs, wait outside for Larry, I told myself. Get out of this room with its reminders. With a sense of urgency, of out-running danger, I hurried from the room, down the stairs, across the foyer and out into the sunlight.

Several minutes later Larry drove up in the Fiat with Phillipe sitting in the rear, tugging at his pipe.

"Look who horned in," Larry said humorously as he reached to open the door for me. But his eyes were apologetic. "Phillipe's been in Switzerland four years and he's never been to Ferney."

"I've never been to the top of the Empire State building," I said lightly, sliding in beside Larry.

"Actually," Phillipe said calmly, "the chateau is only open during July and August, I understand."

"How's everything?" Larry asked casually and grinned. "I haven't seen you in all of two hours."

"Something happened last night—" I hesitated. So Phillipe was here. Larry would tell him, anyway. Phillipe with his scientific interest in everything.

Larry's eyes moved sharply to me while he moved from brake to accelerator.

"Why didn't you tell me before?"

"I couldn't," I reminded. "Lisette came tearing out."

"What happened, Andrea?" he pressed.

"Dad considers it a kind of idiotic prank." I was conscious that Phillipe leaned forward intently, his eyes serious. "Somebody tied together a handful of firecrackers. Those huge ones that really can do damage. And tossed the bundle into my room." I took a deep breath. "There's a hole this big in the carpet." I pantomimed without exaggeration.

"But you weren't hurt?" Phillipe said.

"I wasn't there," I said bluntly. "Dad picked just that moment to knock at my door. The firecrackers landed near the balcony doors."

"First the note, now the firecrackers—and your father persists in believing you are in no danger?" Phillipe was

80

cynical. "He is wrapped in the euphoria of having his daughter at the chateau. But he should be realistic."

"Now wait, Phillipe," Larry said warily. "You're jumping too fast. That note *could* have come from some anti-American crackpot. The firecrackers could have been thrown in by somebody zonked on wine." Larry chuckled. "I'm usually the hothead and you're the one who uses logic."

"Dad's hiring a night watchman," I reported. "Pat was calling a Geneva employment agency today." I tried to sound casual. "The night watchman will be here for a couple of weeks. I'm going with Dad to Copenhagen tomorrow. By the time Dad and I return, the watchman should be on duty."

"I do not expect a night watchman to solve this," Phillipe said, and I turned swiftly to face him. His face was grim. His eyes opaque.

"You think it's someone inside the chateau?" Larry's voice was tense. This was his thought, too, I recalled. "Who in the chateau would want to hurt Andrea? What would be the motive?" From Phillipe he was seeking answers to support this belief.

"You are being logical, Larry," Phillipe chided. Unaware that Larry—and I—felt as he did. "Someone who writes threatening notes, who tosses firecrackers capable of physical injury does not fit into that logical framework."

"Four people in the chateau resent my presence," I conceded. "Claudine, Henri, Pat Fraser—and my grandmother. Henri loathes all Americans, particularly women. Pat Fraser—" I hesitated. "Pat resents my closeness to Dad." I saw the swift exchange between Larry and Phillipe. They knew. "Claudine hates me—I don't know why," I acknowledged. "Perhaps she thinks I'm depriving Lisette of Dad's affection. And Grandmère, whom, of course, I don't suspect, thinks I'm an imposter. Even if she believed me," I forced myself to be honest, "there's a definite hostility towards my mother, which probably would include me as well."

"What about Jeanne? The girl who comes in from the village?" Phillipe prodded.

"No, not Jeanne," I insisted.

"Do not say 'no' to anyone," Phillipe reproved. "Not in a case such as this."

81

"There's something else," I said, my voice so low Phillipe moved forward to hear. "I guess it shook me too much to talk about—"

"Tell us, Andrea," Phillipe ordered. "How can we help without knowing everything?"

"The day I arrived, someone came into my room. I came back to find all the drawers in a mess. The clothes in the closet were pulled down from the hangers, lying in a heap. And on the top," my throat was tight with the recollection, "on the top of the heap lay my best dinner dress, with huge gashes cut into it." Right now I could see that dress. Feel the intent.

"Why didn't you tell me?" Larry was upset. "Phillipe, what does that mean to you?"

"It means," Phillipe said brusquely, "that a psychotic is out to drive Andrea from the chateau. By any means necessary. Even murder. A psychotic masquerading behind normalcy. We must suspect everyone within the chateau, Andrea."

Chapter Eight

"No more talk about the Chateau Laval," Larry said resolutely as we turned onto the auto-route. "We're going to enjoy this afternoon." He turned his head to include Phillipe. A glint in his eye ordering Phillipe to conform.

"Of course," I said with determined gaity. "My first trip into France." For a little while, sitting here beside Larry, I could forget.

I sat back in the Fiat and listened to Larry and Phillipe reminisce about the past school year with increasing respect for Phillipe. My covert hostility was evaporating. He was intensely involved with the children with whom he worked. His book was based on scholarly research that he truly hoped would be of value.

"Andrea, please do not be angry if I am so intrigued with the situation of your mother and yourself," Phillipe said with ingratiating candor. "It is that I am so concerned with the reaction of the children. And the tremendous emotional upheaval later when the father's presence is revealed."

"What he's angling for," Larry intercepted with a grin, "is to persuade you to become a case history in his book."

"All right, Phillipe." I swung about to face him startled that I was capitulating. "I'll be as honest with you as I can." I had survived, gloriously, the shock that my father was still alive. What disturbed me, despite my determination to banish such thoughts from my mind for this afternoon's excursion, was the knowledge that someone at my father's chateau wished me harm.

"Let us talk about Voltaire," Phillipe side-stepped now with exhilaration. "There is a man who fascinates me."

Faster than I anticipated, we were turning off the autoroute at the Geneva Airport exit, following the signs that read "Ferney" and "Paris." We drove through a wide, short tunnel, came out facing what appeared at first sight, surprisingly, to be a tollgate. We drove closer. It was French customs.

"Remind you of the Lincoln Tunnel?" Larry joked as he slowed down to a crawl and reached with one hand for his passport, which rested in an inside pocket of his jacket.

The customs officer asked if we had anything to declare. Larry replied that we had not. I'd reached to pull my passport from my purse while Phillipe produced his. The customs officer dismissed these with a wave of his hand, indicated we were to move ahead.

"You have any idea where the chateau is?" Larry asked Phillipe.

"We'll surely see signs as we approach Ferney," Phillipe said, his eyes scanning the scenery.

We drove slowly, spotted the signs that indicated Ferney was ahead. But we saw no mention of the chateau.

"Okay," Larry decided, "we'll drive straight into Ferney."

We rolled into a small, narrow street, with low shops that had a charming air. Larry pulled up at the curb. Phillipe emerged from the car to go into an antique shop where a pair of Frenchmen argued heatedly but without rancor about local politics. With exquisite courtesy they stopped to listen to Phillipe. He returned to the car with an air of satisfaction.

"Drive down the main street," Phillipe instructed. "This is it," he added with a chuckle. "Not far ahead is a left turn. We take it."

We continued down the street for a short distance, made a sharp left onto a narrow, tree-shaded dirt road. A sign confirmed that this was our destination. I leaned forward eagerly, waiting for the view of Voltaire's chateau.

And then we saw it. Sitting tall behind a wrought-iron fence, surrounded by old shade trees. Buff-colored, three stories high, typical of its period, I guessed.

"Not as grand as I'd expected," Larry said with surprise. "It could be a house in a plush American neighborhood."

"You have seen too many English and Danish palaces," Phillipe chided. "Come," he reached for a rear door of the car. "Let's go have a look."

On the gate an austere sign stated that this was private property and that trespassing would be punished by law. Phillipe had been right about one thing; the chateau was only open to the public during the months of July and August.

We stood before the wrought-iron fence and gazed with interest at the chateau. Behind those walls Voltaire had spent the last years of his life, in freedom and comfort. There he had written his inflammatory pamphlets. There had entertained the great and the near-great of his day.

"That must be the chapel." Phillipe pointed to a small structure at our left. "The chapel that Voltaire maintained was the only church in the world dedicated to God alone. All the others, he said, were dedicated to saints."

"I read somewhere that when the chapel was finished, he asked Rome to send him some sacred relics." I felt such a sense of history, standing here in the golden sunlight, knowing that Voltaire had lived in the chateau just ahead of us. "The Pope sent him a haircloth which had once belonged to St. Francis of Assisi. And on the altar Voltaire put a life-sized statue of Christ, depicted as a sage."

"The inside is probably magnificent," Larry said wistfully. "We'll come another time. On a Saturday afternoon."

We remained for a while, enjoying the beautiful air of tranquillity, such a short distance from the shop-lined main street of Ferney. Then we drove back into town to park before the Voltaire Café and went inside for pastry and coffee. For a little while all my tensions seemed to melt away. I forgot about my locked door in the chateau, the night watchman that was scheduled to parade the grounds against intruders.

On the way back, at Phillipe's insistence, we stopped off at Nyon, built on a hill, to see the old castle that had been a rest camp for Julius Caesar's soldiers and was now a museum. I sensed Phillipe's determination to make me forget, for this afternoon, the ugliness that beset me at the chateau, and I was grateful.

There was a delightful, friendly rivalry between Larry and Phillipe now for my attention, which was flattering. We sat at a sidewalk cafe facing the cluster of sun-dappled plane trees under which the Fiat was parked, while they vied with each other for my approval about projected sightseeing expeditions. I suspected that Larry was slyly trying to persuade me to remain beyond August.

We left Nyon, took a roundabout way back to the auto-route in order to see the small, neat farms that dotted this part of Switzerland. But when we turned off the auto-route at the Rolle exit and headed up the side of the mountain towards the chateau, I felt my throat growing tight.

We stopped briefly in Bougy Villars so that Phillipe might speak with the girl who typed for him. While Larry and I waited in the car, we saw the Bentley roll down the street, returning from Geneva. We trailed behind, Lisette waving enthusiastically when she spotted us.

Larry stopped for a moment to drop off Phillipe, who was now anxious to get to his typewriter. Then we followed the Bentley up the steep incline to the chateau. Heidi spied us, charged forward exuberantly. She greeted Lisette briefly as she emerged from the Bentley, then raced to me.

"Hello, Heidi." I leaned forward affectionately to scratch her behind her huge shaggy ears.

"Lisette, go directly to your room and change," Grandmère ordered. Was there a moment when she was not tense, I wondered pugnaciously. "I wish Claudine to soak that stain from your dress before it sets." Henri was heading now for the garage.

"It was only my lemon ice, Grandmère," Lisette protested, her eyes focused eagerly on Larry and me. She wanted to join us.

"Change, Lisette," Grandmère insisted. "And take Heidi with you before she jumps all over Andrea."

"Did you enjoy Ferney?" Dad dropped an arm about my shoulders while Lisette, with a somber expression, dutifully headed for the door, tugging at Heidi's collar.

"We didn't get inside," Larry said ruefully. "The chateau is open to the public only on Saturday afternoons. We'll have to go another time."

"Of course," Dad agreed briskly. "I do not really see how Andrea can leave at the end of the month." A glint

86

came into his eyes as he exchanged a conspiratorial glance with Larry. "She must see Chamonix and Zermatt. And how can she fly back to the States without seeing Paris?"

"I wouldn't have a job left back at the UN if I stayed here any longer," I laughed.

"You do not have to worry about such things," Dad said quietly, his eyes holding mine. Somehow, I still didn't think of myself as the daughter of a wealthy man. "We will talk about this later, Andrea."

Grandmère, en route to the front door, had heard Dad. She stared at him over one shoulder with a look of shock and fury that chilled me. And then she was walking stiffly into the chateau. Shoulders tense, head high. *Hating me.*

"How was Geneva?" Larry asked Dad.

"How is it always in the summer?" Dad said philsophically. "Overrun with tourists. The streets, the shops, the restaurants—everything is crowded." He shrugged it off, his eyes moving speculatively from Larry to me. I sensed that he was glad that I had found companionship. "Larry, stay for dinner," he said with a persuasive inflection in his voice.

"Not on such short notice," Larry demurred. But the prospect seemed to appeal to him.

"Nonsense. Claudine can always manage one extra for dinner," Dad insisted. "Andrea, please tell Claudine that Larry will be staying. Larry, tell me how you feel about this coming presidential election in your country." Dad relished discussing American politics with Larry, I realized. "Do you believe, as some of your journalists seem to, that the United States is truly entering a new era?"

I hurried into the chateau, delighted that Larry had been invited for dinner, pleased with the relationship between Dad and Larry. Instinct told me that this was not a summer interlude for Larry and me. Though we'd known each other such a very brief time, I knew that Larry would be important in my life.

Upstairs Grandmère was talking to Lisette.

"Lisette, you are dawdling," she rebuked. "Get out of that dress and take it downstairs to Claudine."

Did Lisette remember her mother? She must—she remembered Michel so vividly. Kept him in that secret life of hers. Poor baby, I thought compassionately. What a tragedy it was for her when her mother and Michel died. Of course,

Grandmère loved her deeply, yet there was this painful strictness at every turn.

I walked quickly down the hall towards the kitchen, hearing Claudine talking agitatedly, in French to someone. My mind automatically translated.

"Henri, the girl must leave! We must do something! Anything, Henri!"

"Be quiet, Claudine," Henri reproached in French.

I stopped dead. My mouth went dry. My heart was pounding. Then I swung about, driven away from the sound of those voices and moved noiselessly back down the carpeted corridor. Claudine's words ricocheted through my mind. My instinct was to run immediately to Dad with this. To Dad and Larry. That night watchman was a travesty. The danger to me lay within the chateau. Not from outsiders!

"Andrea—" Lisette leaned over the bannister, her long dark hair falling picturesquely about her face. "Does it make you angry when Heidi jumps upon you?"

"Darling, no," I said with conviction. "You know I adore Heidi."

"She adores you," Lisette said firmly, hurrying towards me. "I have to take this dress out to Claudine so she can soak the stain."

"I'll go with you. I have to tell Claudine that Larry is staying for dinner."

"Oh, super," Lisette said exuberantly. "That's an American word. My roommate, Kathy, uses it all the time."

When Lisette and I returned from our errands, we discovered Dad and Larry had settled themselves in the library. Dad was showing Larry his small collection of rifles, kept in a case at one side of the room.

"I loathe guns," Dad said with candor, "but it is interesting, is it not, that a country that has been free of conflict for over a hundred years insists that every adult male be trained to bear arms." Dad reached forward to pull Lisette to him. She glowed at this display of affection. "Lisette, go to the piano and play for us, please," he ordered. "She plays brilliantly," he said with pride. "Not like a child."

*   *   *

88

We sat down to dinner earlier than normal because Claudine so decreed.

"Sometimes I am not sure who is the mistress of the chateau," Dad chuckled. "Maman or Claudine."

Grandmère frowned her disapproval.

"Claudine is devoted to us all," she reminded him. "But her sense of humor is sometimes weak. Please, Armand, don't speak this way." She gestured for dismissal of this vein of conversation as Henri arrived to serve the roast tenderloin, after Claudine's superb onion soup.

Much of the table talk was about New York, a city Dad recalled with fondness, and for which Larry—like me—had a deep affection.

"I have never been interested in going to the States," Pat contributed with a frown of disdain. "Why, when all of Europe is so close?"

"Grandmère didn't want me to go to New York with Kathy last spring," Lisette reported with an impish grin, "but Dad let me go, and we had a great time. Kathy lives in an apartment high over the park, and at night the lights were so beautiful."

"But not as beautiful as what you see from the chateau at night," Grandmère retorted drily. "Nor from the apartment in Geneva. So you have been to New York," she shrugged.

"You enjoyed shopping on Fifth Avenue, many years ago, Maman," Dad reminded.

Involuntarily my eyes shot to my grandmother. Somehow, I couldn't imagine her in New York. Many years ago, Dad said. Had she known Mother? Had she seen *me?* I gazed at her with fresh awareness. Feeling strangely closer, despite the barrier she'd erected between us.

Grandmère had not expected this reminder from Dad. She had shut a door on those years. Her eyes were filled with anguish. She remembered. Not the days of shopping along Fifth Avenue. But Dad's pain, when Mother disappeared with me.

Suddenly there was an almost unbearable tension about the table. Dad and Grandmère had catapulted back through the years, sharing an experience the rest of us could only imagine. Lisette, so very sensitive, glanced from one to the other a strange, lost look on her small face.

"Americans outside of New York have an absurd way of considering the city a jungle," Larry said with wry amusement. He had intercepted the communication between Dad and Grandmère, was making an effort to bring them back to the present. "And it isn't a jungle at all—any more than any other major city. It just gets a bad press. I miss the city," he acknowledged. "In the midst of all this incredible beauty, I miss my city."

I hardly heard what the others were saying. I'd seen the anguish in my grandmother's eyes. I knew she hated me for the pain I'd brought, inadvertently, to my father. She hated me for the years when he'd longed so passionately for his other child, who had disappeared into nowhere. How could I fight this? How could I make her understand that I, too, had been cheated?

Over the *citeau au kirsch* Dad coaxed Pat into retelling some of the legends of her part of Scotland. He was flatteringly attentive. She spoke with unexpected eloquence. For a few moments she was almost beautiful. But when her gaze by accident clashed with mine, I saw the familiar hostility there. For a little while we had been a casual dinner party. For a little while.

Right after dinner Lisette was dispatched to bed. Pat excused herself with some vague reference to work.

"To listen to Pat you are a slave driver, Armand," Grandmère said with impatience.

"Pat works when it suits her," Dad said, unruffled. "Whenever she wishes, she takes off a few days. Let Pat work in her own fashion." His smile was indulgent. Didn't he know she was in love with him? No, of course he didn't.

Grandmère lingered briefly before making her own excuses. Now Dad, Larry and I went outdoors to sit on the redwood chairs lined up at the favorite observation point. Each night I marveled afresh at the magnificence of the view.

We sat wrapped in darkness, enjoying the fragrance of the country air, while below us—beyond the vineyards—moved the sparse night traffic of the auto-route. Beyond the auto-route Lake Geneva was touched with moonlight. The lights of France across the water, the lights of Morges, Lausanne to our left, Geneva to our right.

Down below in the stillness of the night we could hear the erratic typing from Pat's room. Somewhere, a dog barked sharply. Every sound was magnified here on the mountainside.

"Did you know?" Larry said reminiscently, his gaze focused on the redwood chair in which he sat, "that in a park in Geneva there are a group of transplanted California redwoods? The tour guides on the buses always point them out."

"Ah, yes," Dad said emphatically. "There is far too much for you to see in one month, Andrea."

I laughed. But I remembered Grandmère's fury when Dad had pursued this topic at the dinner table. I remembered Claudine's agitated voice. "Henri, the girl must leave! We must do something! Anything, Henri!" And I had said nothing to Dad about this. Nor to Larry. *Why didn't I tell them?*

Larry began to yawn and apologized.

"All this fresh mountain air," he said, rising to his feet. "I don't know how Phillipe can work at night."

"I think it is time for all of us to go to bed," Dad decided. "Tomorrow," he reminded me, "we leave at 12:20 for Copenhagen. We must be in the car, en route for the airport, by 10:45."

Larry took off in the Fiat for the short run to his house. Dad and I went inside. Dad locked the front door for the night, and together we started up the stairs. With each step my mind ordered me to tell Dad what I had overheard between Claudine and Henri. Yet I couldn't.

With cowardice, I made up my mind to wait until after Copenhagen, when Dad and I would have had a chance to be alone together for a stretch of time. Despite the instant closeness between us, what did we know of each other? How could I make such an accusation against Claudine and Henri, whom he had known so long and who were almost part of the family?

"Sleep well, Andrea," Dad said affectionately at my door. "If you are not awake by ten, I will see that Jeanne calls you."

"I'll be awake," I promised. "Good night, Dad."

I let myself into my room with the realization that the door had been unlocked all day. My heart pounding, I reached for the wall switch. Swiftly, my eyes scanned the room. Apparently, everything was as I'd left it earlier.

I crossed quickly to the windows, after I'd locked the door to my room, to make sure these were locked, that the French doors to the balcony were locked. I drew the draperies tight against the night feeling a spurious security.

Wasting no time I prepared for bed. Yet hesitating about plunging my room into darkness. Then suddenly I was alert. What was that at my door?

I inched forward. My eyes focused on the door. No sign, yet, of anyone trying to dislodge the key. I could scream, I told myself. The whole floor would hear me. And then, absurdly, relief swept through me. I went to the door, turned the key, pulled the door wide.

"Heidi, what are you doing out here?" I chided. "You're supposed to be with Lisette!"

But Heidi waddled into my room, and sank to the floor with a thud. Her head turned to me, huge brown eyes asking that I fondle her.

"Oh, Heidi, what am I going to do with you?" I locked the door again, crossed to where she lay, and dropped to my haunches. My hands stroked her plush thick fur. It was only Heidi making faint sounds at the door, and I'd been so frightened! "All right, you can stay," I soothed, when she put her head down as though prepared for permanent residence. Actually, I was glad that Heidi was here. "Be a good girl," I said sternly, wanting to say, "Heidi, *watch*." But nobody would come into my room tonight without Heidi raising an outcry.

From sheer exhaustion—and relieved because Heidi was here—I fell asleep almost immediately.

* * *

I awoke with a start. With a sense of falling through space. Not, for a moment, grasping my whereabouts. Not immediately identifying the frenzied screams close by.

Lisette! I sat upright with a shock of recognition. Heidi was whining at the door. Guiltily I realized Heidi belonged in the next room with Lisette.

"Heidi, wait!" My hands shook. I reached at the foot of

my bed for my robe not bothering to switch on the lamp. In the darkness, I ran barefoot, to the door.

I pulled the door wide, charged into the hall, Heidi at my heels. Dad was rushing forward from his room.

"It's Lisette." He reached for the door to her room. "Andrea, stay out here."

Dad pulled the door wide, and rushed inside, followed by Heidi. Ignoring his admonitions, I followed him into the room, switched on the lights. Lisette lay huddled against her pillow, crying in wracking gasps.

"Lisette! Lisette, darling—" Dad reached to pull her to him. "What is it? Did you have a bad dream?"

"Someone came into my room—" Lisette's voice was foggy with shock. "I woke up. I couldn't see his face, just the pillow in his hands—" She shivered in recall. I saw the pillow on the floor beside Lisette's bed, and turned cold. "When I screamed, he went out through the balcony." The doors still wide. The night air chill.

Grandmère swept into the room white, trembling, striving to offer a facade of calm.

"What is it? What has happened to Lisette? Armand, what happened?"

"She is all right, Maman," Dad soothed, rocking Lisette in his arms. Six years ago Michel died. Now Lisette was especially precious. I could hear Claudine and Henri hurrying down from their third floor quarters as Dad talked to Grandmère. Henri was impatient with Claudine's near-hysteria. "There was an intruder."

Grandmère's eyes fastened hypnotically to the pillow on the floor.

"What did he want? Why didn't Heidi attack him? She never even barked!"

"Heidi was with me," I explained, my face hot as Grandmère's eyes fastened accusingly on me. "She was scratching on my door—I let her in."

"It was someone—deranged," Dad said carefully. "But tomorrow night there will be a watchman on duty. Henri will be on guard with a gun for the balance of the night."

"Lisette—" I leaned compassionately towards her. She was quiet now, but clinging to Dad. "Would you like to spend the rest of the night in my room? In my bed?"

"With you?" Lisette asked solemnly.
"With me, darling," I promised her.

* * *

Later—much later—I still lay wide awake thinking about the intruder in Lisette's room. Not in pursuit of me, but of Lisette. He knew my room. No mistake, this. Now there were two quarries. Lisette and me.

This was a whole new ball game.

Chapter Nine

I awoke to find Lisette still sound asleep at the edge of the bed. Clutching a pillow, her legs jackknifed beneath her. Poor baby. What a dreadful scare last night.

I leaned over her for a view of the clock. Past nine. I must dress. I left the bed as quietly as I could, collected my clothes, went into the bathroom.

Dad and I would undoubtedly be leaving as scheduled. He'd said nothing last night about a switch in plans. Yes. Dad had business in Copenhagen. Perhaps it was best not to put too much importance on last night. Lisette was such an imaginative child. We shouldn't appear too upset about the intruder.

I dressed, moved as quietly as possible from the room confident that Lisette would sleep until noon. Walking down the stairs, I heard Dad talking with Pat in his office. Pat must have taken another sleeping pill last night. By now she knew about Lisette. She'd be terribly upset.

As I reached the foyer, Dad emerged from the office. His face lighted as he spied me turning into the hall.

"Ah, bright and early, Andrea. We will have breakfast together."

"Dad, do you think I shouldn't go along with you?" I asked uneasily. "Do you suppose Lisette will feel better if I stay?" She'd been so disappointed at not being allowed to go along with us.

Dad hesitated briefly.

"No. You will go with me, Andrea," he said firmly. "Her

grandmother is here. Pat is here. Claudine and Henri. Lisette will be fine. And tonight an armed guard will be on duty." Again, his face was strained. "I cannot understand these happenings. There must be someone deranged on the loose." Last night Dad had said that. "It has already been reported to the police." He shrugged. "How can they find the man? There is no lead."

We had a leisurely breakfast in the family dining room. I knew, from Jeanne's tense expression, that she had heard about last night. While we lingered over a second cup of coffee, Dad instructed Jeanne to have Henri bring the car around front.

"Poor Henri was on guard duty until daybreak," Dad said sympathetically. "But he will be able to catch up on his sleep tonight."

I went upstairs again for the light coat Dad had ordered me to take along. Lisette still slept soundly. Her face tear-stained, poignantly lovely. I brushed the sweep of dark hair from her face, covered her lightly. because there was a briskness in the air this morning. With my weekender, coat, and shoulder bag in tow, I tiptoed from the room, hurried downstairs to meet Dad.

The Bentley was out front, Henri behind the wheel. Dad and I settled ourselves on the back seat. As we moved down the driveway, out onto the public road, my eyes moved to the small, pink house below. What would Larry and Phillipe think about last night? Whom were we to view with suspicion?

Everyone in the chateau had come charging forward at the sound of Lisette's screams. No one could have been in Lisette's room, managed to get out, and back inside the chateau in that brief interval between screams and appearances. Everybody was there at Lisette's door. Except Pat Fraser.

Suddenly I was aware that Henri stared at my reflection in the rear view mirror. Stared with a contained fury in his eyes that unnerved me. I tried to pull my gaze away, to listen to what Dad was saying about Copenhagen.

What was happening at the chateau? Why these attacks, first on me, now on Lisette? Could they be distinctly separate, perpetrated by two different people? No, the odds were against that.

96

I couldn't believe that Henri and Claudine, who adored Lisette, could in any way be involved with last night. Physically this was impossible, my mind reasoned. Pat? Pat, too, was devoted to Lisette. Seemingly devoted. But why this hatred on Claudine's and Henri's part towards me?

Was Claudine afraid something was going to happen to me—and this would be trouble for the family? What did she know that Dad—and I—didn't know? Why had she said, "Henri, the girl must leave! We must do something! Anything, Henri!" *What did she mean?*

"We will check into the Palace Hotel," Dad said. "I will go to my business meeting. You will have three hours or so to shop. We will change money at the airport," he said with an indulgent chuckle. "Buy something pretty for Lisette. Something she can take with her to school. Sweaters, perhaps," he decided. Now he was somber. "I wish Lisette could go to school in Geneva, so she could live at home."

"Why can't she?" I asked impetuously. "There are such fine schools in Geneva."

"Your Grandmère," he said philosophically. "No school is quite right for Lisette in her eyes. She had been so devoted to Lisette these last six years. I must allow her to make these decisions."

At the airport we had only a brief wait before our flight was announced.

"Let us go directly to the boarding gate," Dad said. "On inter-European flights seats are not assigned."

We settled ourselves in seats that would provide us with excellent views. Especially important on this flight, Dad said with satisfaction, because we would be flying over the Alps. Almost immediately after take-off the stewardesses began to serve our cold lunch. Dad talked nostalgically as we ate about his years in New York when I was a baby. The time sped by.

The captain announced that we were flying over Germany.

"Soon," Dad said, "we'll be landing at the Copenhagen Airport. We're scheduled to arrive at 2:15."

We landed as scheduled and took a taxi from the airport to the Palace Hotel. I was fascinated by the hordes of people on the Vesterbrogade. There were tourists of all nations along with the Danes. The young predominated; they were dressed in dungarees and faded shirts and sandals, with packs on their backs, maps in their hands.

We registered in the quietly elegant lobby of the Palace, sent our bags up to our rooms, and walked to the entrance to the Strøget.

"You cannot get lost here," he chuckled. "The Strøget is a mile-long pedestrian mall." He was pulling bills from his wallet as he talked. "Walk as far as you like. Shop along the way. When you have had enough of walking, turn around and head back for the hotel. Here on the Strøget you will get a marvelous flavor of Copenhagen. I will meet you for dinner at the Palace Hotel restaurant at seven o'clock. All right, Andrea?" His eyes were faintly anxious.

"I'll be there," I promised, touched that he was concerned for me. Mother was one to trust to providence. And then my eyes widened in astonishment at the wad of bills Dad was thrusting into my hands. "I won't spend anything like that, Dad!"

"Try," he laughed, pleased at my astonishment. "There are places, when you are tired, where you can go in for coffee and pastry. I will see you at seven," he reiterated. "You do not mind my leaving you this way?"

"No, Dad," I insisted, and leaned forward to kiss him lightly.

I waited while he climbed into a taxi, then entered the Strøget, immediately intrigued by the air of conviviality in the area. People of all ages, all nations moved leisurely along the mall. Small, colorful shops lined both sides. Jewelry, souvenirs, sweaters, clothing, bakery products—everything was available.

I stopped in a tiny jewelry shop, drawn by their window display of necklaces. Inside, where a salesgirl spoke English, I found a hammered silver pendant on a chain, depicting a Hans Christian Andersen fairy-tale character. Perfect for Lisette, I decided with pleasure. On impulse I bought twin pendants for Jeanne and myself. For a girl who had never been more than five miles from home, I thought sentimentally, a gift from Copenhagen would hold special value.

I strolled slowly up the Strøget, stopping again at the Rosenthal china store, impressively large compared to the

98

usual small shops. I bought a charming set of glasses, to be mailed back to the apartment in New York.

I went into a restaurant for a pot of tea and a pastry, reveling in the multi-lingual conversations that flourished all about me. Suddenly I felt oddly chilled when a newcomer, who was astonishingly like Henri, sat at the table directly in front of me. I'd hoped, for these few hours, to put the chateau completely out of my mind.

More rapidly than I'd anticipated, I vacated my table in the restaurant. The resemblance of the man at the next table to Henri unnerved me. Don't think about the chateau, I chastised myself. This was a special holiday.

I forced myself to feel interest in the sweater shops I passed, finally deciding to shop at the Sweater House, a tiny, delightful sweater boutique with an open, winding staircase going to the stamp-sized second floor. Here I bought extravagantly for Lisette and myself, visualizing Lisette's face when she saw her gifts, still feeling guilty that I had left her behind.

Farther along I dallied in the Royal Copenhagen store, moving from floor to floor with a vague thought of buying something for Grandmère. Grandmère and Pat, I decided. Perhaps, I told myself with ill-founded optimism, a gift might bridge the gap between us.

For Pat, who liked to have coffee at her desk when she worked, I bought an exquisite, shockingly expensive, two-cup coffee pot. For Grandmère, who always had breakfast in her room, a dramatic breakfast tray. Waiting for my gifts to be wrapped, I checked my watch. Time to start back in the direction of the hotel.

I arrived at the Palace Hotel shortly before seven. Dad stood waiting just inside the lobby.

"You have shopped," he said with a complacent smile, reaching for my packages. "Let me take these to the desk and have them sent up to your room."

"What a lovely idea." I was relieved to relinquish the spoils of my shopping.

I waited at the entrance to the restaurant, pleasantly conscious of hunger. Tonight I would be able to walk into my room without alarm. I could turn off the lamps and sleep without that sense of unease that was part of my life at the chateau.

Dad returned to me. We walked together into the elegant restaurant. It was a long, high-ceilinged room, lushly carpeted, was lighted by an array of dramatic chandeliers. The tables were elegantly set, with red leather upholstered armchairs grouped about them. Enormously tall windows looked out on the square.

The service was impeccable and the food delicious. Dad ordered an American dinner. I chose Danish food. Dad proved himself a charming dinner conversationalist, determined to make this a memorable occasion for me.

"After dinner we will go across to Tivoli. It is five minutes away," Dad said in high humor. "This is one of the showplaces of Europe." Quite unexpectedly, his face was serious. "Andrea, I have been thinking about this unpleasantness at the chateau. When we return, I will consult a firm of private detectives." He signed. "Your grandmother will be upset. They will come in and ask a lot of questions. I remember when Michel and his mother died. It was dreadful, having the police come in, asking us so many painful questions."

"But their deaths were accidental, weren't they?" I stared at Dad in shock.

"Even with accidental death, the police must investigate," Dad reminded me unhappily.

Suddenly I felt compelled to talk about it.

"It was a boating accident, wasn't it?" Why did I question Dad this way, I chastised myself. *He didn't want to talk about it.*

"Six years ago this month." Suddenly Dad seemed exhausted. "We were at the summer house. I had just bought a new boat. An exact replica of the old one because the children adored it. Henri was to repair the old one so we would have a spare. They sat together at the dock, the old one freshly painted to duplicate the new. A red flag of warning on the one which was not seaworthy. But somehow, during the night, the flag was removed. Michel and his mother got into the boat—the one which was not seaworthy. She was wearing dark glasses against the strong sun— she didn't recognize the fresh paint." Dad took a deep breath. "Henri heard them cry out. He took the other boat and rushed to them. But it was too late. He could do nothing. For three days Henri was drunk."

"How awful," I said in a shocked whisper.

"Lisette was in bed with a cold. Otherwise, she, too, would have gone down with her mother and Michel. This is why, sometimes, we seem to spoil Lisette. It is a miracle that we still have her."

It was difficult to resume our air of festivity, though we both tried desperately to recapture our earlier mood. We lingered over dessert and coffee until Dad announced it was time we left for Tivoli.

"But first you must go upstairs to your room for your coat," Dad ordered. "It will be cool this evening."

We stood in line for our tickets, hearing the exuberant orchestral music inside. Much laughter about us. Everyone with an air of anticipation. Just as we passed through the gates into the vast acreage of Tivoli Gardens, the vari-colored lights were switched on.

Hand in hand we wandered about, admiring the flowers, the light-bathed fountains, the exotic restaurants, the much patronized rides. We sat before the open stage and enjoyed the fantastic, free entertainment. We drank coffee at a terrace cafe and admired the marvelous pagoda with its thousands of lights. All this, I thought with awe, in the heart of a city.

Not until the lights began to dim in preparation for the midnight closing, did Dad and I leave Tivoli to walk the brief distance to our hotel.

"You have not been to Copenhagen if you have not been to Tivoli," Dad said complacently. "I have ordered a car with a driver for tomorrow at ten. We will be able to sight-see until lunchtime. Then we will head for the airport. In the morning I only have to make an early phone call, and then my business is completed."

I slept soundly, feeling so safe in my hotel room, that I didn't wake until my travel clock alarm jingled gently in my ears. I remembered that Dad had hired a chauffeured car to drive us today.

I was dressed, taking my coat down from the closet, when Dad knocked.

"We will check out, have breakfast, and pick up the car," he said ebulliently. "All right, Andrea?"

At ten o'clock sharp we were at the hotel entrance, just as our rented car arrived. For three hours we drove about

Copenhagen, to the Amelienborg Palace, residence of the Danish King; the Royal Theatre; the Gefion Fountain; the Langelinie Promenade, where we saw the famous statue of Little Mermaid sitting on a boulder at the water's edge. Then Dad decided it was time for lunch, after which we'd head for the airport.

"Have you enjoyed this trip?" Dad asked searchingly while we ate heartily of Danish smorgasbord.

"It's been delightful." I smiled reassuringly. He seemed so anxious.

"It has upset me," he said with candor, "that your welcome has been tainted with such unpleasantness. I wished everything to be perfect for you, Andrea."

"Grandmère is unhappy that I came," I said softly, and immediately was sorry because Dad seemed so distressed.

"That is because she does not yet know you," he said. "Please, Andrea, give her time."

"I have sent to New York for my birth certificate," I admitted. "Perhaps when she sees it, she'll believe I'm her granddaughter." I hesitated. "But she hated my mother, didn't she?"

"There was not a good relationship," Dad said slowly. "Actually, they never even met. When Maman came to New York for ten days to visit us, your mother picked up and went off with you to stay with a cousin in Wisconsin. Maman was dreadfully upset at the break-up of the marriage. She knew what it meant to me to lose you." Dad forced a smile, reached a hand across the table to cover mine. "But that is all over now. We have found each other again. And your grandmother will learn to love you as she loves Lisette. Please, Andrea, give her time."

* * *

On the flight back to Geneva Dad talked much about Michel. Not until now did I realize today was the sixth anniversary of that tragic accident. Grandmère, I thought with compassion, would remember the day. Lisette was too young.

Right on schedule we landed at the Geneva Airport. Henri was waiting with the Bentley at the parking lot. He lounged against the hood of the car, with a strained expression. He, too, would remember the date. Dad had said that after the accident Henri was drunk for three days.

Did Henri blame himself for not being able to save Michel and his mother? *Or was he responsible for the red danger flag being removed?*

Henri was taciturn as we settled ourselves in the car. Dad, too, seemed preoccupied, despite his efforts at conversation. On the auto-route I pretended deep interest in the scenery to release him from the need to talk.

Grandmère must have heard the car approaching the chateau. She was at the entrance as Henri pulled to a stop.

"Was it hot in Copenhagen?" Grandmère asked. "It can be as bad as Geneva, I recall."

"It was hot," Dad conceded with a wry smile. His eyes searched Grandmère's face. She seemed tense, anxious as she stood before us. "Is everything all right here?"

"Now it is." Grandmère paused. Fighting, I suspected, for that outward calm she treasured. But this hesitancy alarmed both Dad and me.

"What happened?" Dad pressed.

"Last night—in the middle of the night, really—Lisette decided she wanted a glass of milk. Claudine had served filet of sole for dinner, and Lisette was thirsty. She—she fell down almost the whole flight of stairs."

"Is she all right?" Dad was pale with shock.

"She's fine," Grandmère reassured him. "Just shaken up a bit. Pat was marvelous," Grandmère reported conscientiously. "She took complete charge. She insisted Dr. Gautier come out immediately. Lisette is just bruised. No broken bones, no sprains. But I was so frightened." For a moment Grandmère seemed a terrified old lady. "Seeing her lying that way, unconscious, at the foot of the stairs."

"Dr. Gautier is sure there's no need for X-rays?" Dad, too, sought to remain calm. "How long was she unconscious?"

"For only a few moments, Armand," Grandmère soothed. "I'd heard her door open—I hadn't been sleeping —but by the time I'd pulled on my robe and walked out into the corridor, she had already fallen."

"I'll go up to see her." A pulse hammered furiously in Dad's forehead.

"She's asleep," Grandmère stopped him. "Later you'll go

up to see her." She paused. "Lisette—Lisette said that Michel pushed her down the stairs. Armand, why does she play these awful games?"

But it wasn't Michel who'd pushed Lisette down the stairs. She was pushed by someone very much alive! Whoever was in Lisette's room with a pillow. Whoever had tossed those firecrackers into my room. Whoever had shoved the note beneath my door—and slashed my dress.

"Maman, what about the night watchman? Was he on duty last night?" Dad asked carefully.

"No. There was some mix-up. Pat tells me he will arrive this evening." Her eyes were opaque. What was she thinking?

Dad suspected, as I did, that it was a very earthly push that sent fragile little Lisette tumbling down those stairs. Someone who managed to escape, in the few moments between the time he shoved Lisette to what might have been her death and the moment Grandmère emerged from her room.

Couldn't Dad understand that the night watchman could not have stopped this? Someone within the chateau wished Lisette dead. Wished *me* dead. Dad's two surviving children. *Why.*

Chapter Ten

Just before dinner Dad and I went in to see Lisette, who seemed so small and pale in bed. But she threw her arms hungrily about Dad when he leaned over to kiss her.

"I've got bruises all over," she said dramatically. "I could have been killed."

Dad flinched. I bent forward quickly to kiss her.

"Darling, don't say that," I said with reproach, hugging her anxiously as her slim arms closed about my neck with fervor.

"Grandmère says you are being allowed downstairs tomorrow," Dad said. "Andrea—" he turned to me with a conspiratorial wink, "do you think we ought to wait until she is downstairs before you give her the presents you bought in Copenhagen?"

"Now!" Lisette clamored. "Please, father, now!"

I went to my room for the pendant and the two sweaters I had bought for Lisette. She was shiny-eyed with pleasure as she inspected each.

"Next week," I promised, "we'll go into Geneva together and have lunch at Perle du Lac." I was so grateful that Lisette had not been seriously injured.

We remained with Lisette until Henri came up to tell us that dinner was about to be served. Now I went into my room to collect the gifts I'd bought for Grandmère and Pat. All at once I felt self-conscious at the prospect of presenting them.

Pat and Grandmère were still in the library, talking to

Dad while he had a predinner cocktail. What he called his American vice. Pat was astonished that I had brought her a gift from Copenhagen. I sensed that, despite the show of pleasure, she would have preferred that I had not made this gesture.

Grandmère, evincing deep admiration for the tray, was oddly wary. I guessed she was deeply pleased by my gesture, yet she would not allow herself to show more than perfunctory approval.

It was strange to sit down to dinner without Lisette at the table. Grandmère was still unnerved from Lisette's brush with disaster on the eve of the anniversary of the drowning of Lisette's mother and brother. Even Pat seemed upset.

"I like the way you are wearing your hair today, Andrea." Dad gazed intently at me while Henri served the chicken in wine sauce.

"It was so hot in Copenhagen," I reminded him. "I pulled it back this way to be cooler."

"Maman, do you realize that Andrea is the image of you at her age?" he asked softly. "Those photographs of you in one of the albums—as a bride. Andrea could be you except that your hair was darker."

"Do you think so?" Grandmère was disconcerted.

"I saw right away, of course, the strong resemblance to Lisette and Michel. But even more strongly, Maman," he continued with triumph, "I see the resemblance to you. After dinner we will look at the photographs in the album. Pat, you will be the judge."

Pat was striving desperately to conceal her distaste for this conversation. She hated me. She didn't want to believe I was Dad's daughter. Did she hate Lisette, too, beneath all that show of devotion? Did she hate everyone Dad loved?

For the first time, I realized, Grandmère began to consider that I might not be an imposter. She was stirred by the possibility that I might, indeed, be her granddaughter. The barrier between us was suddenly precarious.

My birth certificate would arrive, and no doubt would linger in her mind, I promised myself. Grandmère would accept me as Lisette's half sister. Her granddaughter. We would be a whole family.

"Pat is going to make frames for those paintings Lisette did of the lake last week." Grandmère was deliberately diverting the conversation. Also, she was trying to show friendship for Pat because Pat had been so efficient when Lisette had fallen down the stairs. "Lisette is delighted."

"I enjoy working with wood," Pat said. "And it is not difficult at all." She shot a small, vindictive glance at me.

"You made a beautiful tobacco box for me several years ago," Dad recalled flatteringly. "I still have it on my night table."

"My grandfather, a stubborn old Scotsman if there ever was one, taught me to make these things when I was a child. Younger than Lisette." Color touched her cheeks because Dad had mentioned the tobacco box. But her eyes, when they settled on me, were cold steel. Grandmère might be on the verge of accepting me, but not Pat Fraser.

All through dinner I was conscious of Grandmère's eyes roving covertly to me. Appraising. Reassessing. I didn't mind. I felt a kind of exhilaration because I believed she was moving closer to accepting me, intrigued by Dad's suggestion that I was a younger replica of herself.

Dad, too, was aware of Grandmère's compulsive scrutiny. A small, pleased smile telling me he had deliberately plotted this bit of intrigue. Were Grandmère and I truly so similar? It was difficult for me to tell.

After dinner Dad marshalled us all into the library so that he could pull forth the family album which dated back to the early years of Grandmère's marriage. Pat was restless, irritated at being drawn into this scene as an arbitrator.

"I should get my filing up to date," she said tightly, sitting at the edge of the sofa, while Dad thumbed through the album. "This time of night the office is quiet. There are no telephone interruptions."

"Relax tonight, Pat," Dad ordered her with good humor. "I want you to look at this particular photograph and tell them what you think." He was squinting at a page in the scrapbook. "Here," he said with triumph. "This photograph of Maman in the first year of her marriage. Could this not be Andrea? I defy anyone to deny the resemblance."

"Armand," Maman chided, "don't put words into Pat's mouth."

Dad rose from his chair, crossed to sit between Pat and me on the sofa, the scrapbook resting on his knees. He pointed to a snapshot of Grandmère. Both Pat and I leaned forward intently.

The resemblance was dramatic. Even I could see it. I was mesmerized. My eyes were riveted to the photograph of Grandmère in an elegant dress fashionable fifty years earlier.

"Yes." Pat's voice was dry. "There seems to be a marked resemblance."

Quite early both Grandmère and Pat decided it was time to retire.

"We had little sleep last night," Pat said with faint accusation, as though Dad and I had no right to enjoy ourselves in Copenhagen at such a critical time.

"I know," Dad said compassionately. Unaware of—or ignoring—her air of accusation. "Andrea and I will go up shortly, too. I will look in on Lisette before I go to my room." He hesitated. "Where is Heidi? She was not with Lisette earlier."

"I put her outside last night," Pat said. "I thought it might be advisable to have a dog about the grounds." She paused. "You were away. Henri would sleep through a bomb."

"Lisette did not object to having Heidi away?" Dad chuckled. "Usually there is trouble."

"It took some persuasion," Pat conceded. "I reminded her that Heidi is a mountain dog. She needs some nights out in the fresh air." Pat's voice softened. "Lisette's sense of drama accepted this. Would you prefer that Heidi be in the room with Lisette?"

"Do not bother tonight," Dad said casually. "Tomorrow I will bring Heidi back into the house."

What a shame, I thought, that Heidi had not been with Lisette last night. If she had been, whoever shoved Lisette down those stairs would be considerably roughed up now, I realized with frustration. We'd actually been so close to nailing the culprit.

"I'm going to have another glass of wine," Dad decided when we were alone. "Have a glass with me," he coaxed. "It will help you fall asleep."

"I doubt that I'll have much trouble tonight," I laughed, but my smile was an acceptance. "Is the night watchman on duty tonight?" I asked with curiosity while Dad poured wine for us.

"Yes. I spoke with him earlier." Dad's eyes were anxious again. "There will be no intruder tonight."

We drank our wine slowly, talking about the Copenhagen trip. Then together we left the library and headed upstairs. We could hear Henri moving about the chateau closing up for the night. The windows were locked, the shutters drawn tight, even with a night watchman on duty.

Dad said good night to me at my room, moved on to look in on Lisette. Inside my room I went to the drawer where I kept my key—utilized now only at night—to lock myself in. I crossed to the windows to make sure each was locked, paused to gaze out into the night.

Below I spied the night watchman, a short, stocky man who walked the grounds with a revolver at his waist. Directly below my window Heidi sprawled, puppylike, on the grass. I wished, wistfully, that Heidi were here in my room. Still, I continued to feel with certainty that disaster threatened me—and now Lisette—not from an intruder, but from someone who lived within the chateau.

* * *

When I left my room to go downstairs to breakfast, I could hear Dad talking with Lisette in her room. I gathered they were having breakfast together there. Lisette sounded exuberant about this arrangement.

In the kitchen Claudine was shrieking at Jeanne for taking too long with the morning breakfast trays. She wanted Jeanne to prepare vegetables for a salad for luncheon. I suspected that Jeanne had not taken too long at all. Claudine, devoted to Lisette, was still unnerved about Lisette's tumble down the stairs.

"*Bonjour.*" I forced a smile as I hovered in the kitchen doorway.

"*Bonjour, Mademoiselle,*" A bright, eager smile from Jeanne.

"*Bonjour, Mademoiselle,*" Claudine parroted stiffly.

"Would you like breakfast on the terrace?" Jeanne asked. "It is a beautiful morning."

"Lovely, Jeanne," I approved. "Just a croissant and coffee."

I determinedly cut through the kitchen door, which Claudine must lock directly behind me. I knew, from the vigor with which she closed the door that she was still annoyed with this security measure. And I was still nervous about the things she said which I couldn't comprehend.

I settled myself on the terrace, leaned back in my chair, and allowed my gaze to rest on the sweep of lake and mountains.

Jeanne came out to the terrace with a plate of croissants and a small carafe of coffee. I dug into my jacket pocket to pull forth the tiny box with the pendant I'd bought for her.

"I thought you might like this, Jeanne," I said casually as I extended the box. "I bought one exactly like it for myself."

"Oh, Mademoiselle!" She took the box, her eyes wide with amazement. "Why do you do this for me?" Already she was pulling away the wrappings.

"Because I like you," I laughed.

Jeanne lifted the pendant from the box as though it might have been a precious stone. Her eyes were rapt with admiration.

"*Merci*," she said earnestly. "I will take it with me when I go away to school." Suddenly there was something new in her eyes. Curiosity. Envy. "How good it must be to be rich." For a moment hostility there in her eyes.

"Jeanne!" Claudine's voice shot imperiously through the morning quiet. "*Ici!*"

Hastily Jeanne stuffed the tiny box and the wrappings into one pocket of her uniform, dropped the pendant into another.

"*Merci, Mademoiselle,*" she murmured again, and with a swift, parting smile she darted towards the kitchen door.

My eyes sought out the small, pink house below. My heart pounded as I watched Larry bring out a tray and move its contents to the round, white, umbrella-shaded table on their small patio. With tray in hand he went back inside the house. I could hear, faintly, the sound of music from the stereo.

No tutoring today. It was Saturday, I recalled. But there must have been no tutoring yesterday, either, with Lisette kept in bed.

What did Larry think about what happened? Suddenly I

110

was deeply curious about Larry's and Phillipe's reaction.

In a few moments Larry came out again. I saw him turn to glance up at the chateau. He spied me. Waved. Walked to the edge of the road below.

"Come on down for coffee," he called. "A second cup," he amplified, realizing I was at breakfast.

"In a few moments," I called back.

I covered the remaining croissants with a napkin, against the tiny bugs that came from the vineyards, turned my cup upside down so that the sweetness would not draw further bugs, and started down the driveway to the steep incline that would take me down to the house below.

"How was Copenhagen?" Larry greeted me with a broad smile.

"Marvelous." How good it was to be standing here with Larry.

"Try Phillipe's coffee. It's fabulous. I do all the same things, but the result is different."

I sat down at the table. Larry poured for me, his eyes saying much. Inside I could hear the steady noise of the typewriter. The stereo was silenced now.

"You know about Lisette?" My eyes held his.

"Yes." Larry was serious. "Pat Fraser came down to tell me yesterday morning, before it was time for me to show. Andrea, what really happened?" His eyes questioning. Skeptical.

"What did Pat tell you?"

"That Lisette had left her room in the middle of the night for a drink, and that she took a bad spill down the stairs."

"Lisette said that Michel pushed her," I reported feeling cold inside. "She keeps Michel as a fantasy playmate. I'm sure she was pushed. But not by a figment of her imagination."

"First the intruder in her room. Now this. It looks as though the attacker has taken a new direction."

"I don't want to be safe at the cost of Lisette's life!"

"How does your grandmother—and your father—feel about this?" Larry asked.

"Both of them feel, inwardly, that someone shoved Lisette down the stairs, though the last time Grandmère mentioned it," I acknowledged, "she intimated that Lisette

111

tripped. Dad asked right away about the night watchman."

"That's right. What about the night watchman?"

"He wasn't there. There was some mix-up, Pat said. She'd hired him to begin on Thursday evening. Instead, he began last night."

"I've got this radar that tells me the night watchman's being on duty would not have prevented what happened to Lisette," Larry said bluntly. "But I don't suppose your father or grandmother will accept that?"

"They're both upset. I don't know what they actually think." I reached determinedly for the cup of coffee before me. "You're right. Phillipe's coffee is terrific."

"What about private detectives?" Larry was intent on probing further.

"Dad said he would consult a firm. He was unhappy because Grandmère is going to be terribly upset when they come in and start asking questions."

"Better Grandmère upset than Lisette or you murdered," Larry said drily. "When is he calling in the detectives?"

"The first of the week, I assume. He can't do anything over the weekend."

Phillipe walked out onto the patio, cup in hand.

"I follow the carafe of coffee," he said amiably. "How are you, Andrea?" The question was casual, but his eyes were probing as he sat at the table and reached for the carafe.

"I'm fine. And Lisette is recuperating nicely." I said with some defensiveness, never having quite abandoned my belief that he disliked my half sister.

"I'd feel better if you took Lisette and went into Geneva to stay at the apartment," Larry said honestly. "Until the detectives come up with some answers."

"No," Phillipe said sharply, and both Larry and I stared in astonishment. "Stay here at the chateau, Andrea. Find out here who is making these attempts on your life and Lisette's. He—or she—is growing careless. That was a badly planned attempt—probably on impulse, to throw Lisette down the stairs." It *had* to be someone within the chateau, I felt. "How is it that Heidi did not attack him?"

"Heidi was outside, roaming about the grounds," I explained, my mind suddenly jogging to conclusions.

112

"Who put Heidi outside?" Phillipe demanded.

"Pat." My throat was tight. Pat, who had arranged for the night watchman, *who showed up a day late.* "Pat arranged for Heidi to be out of the chateau."

Chapter Eleven

"You did not have time to go on the World of Tomorrow tour in Copenhagen, did you?" Phillipe asked me.

"No. Dad rented a car and we spent the morning visiting major tourist attractions."

I understood Phillipe didn't wish to pursue the possibility that Pat Fraser hated me enough to want to harm me because the evidence was so slight. He questioned, too, instinct told me, that she could be responsible for the attack on Lisette, whom she adored. Or was that affection a pretense? Did Pat Fraser loathe everyone who was close to Dad?

"The tour takes you into Gladsaxe, a suburb of Copenhagen where you see how a small local authority cares for its citizens from cradle to grave. You see the marvelous kindergartens for children of different ages. The really beautiful and practical nursing home for the elderly. Their school is built and equipped according to the most modern principles."

"And they pay a tax rate that would stagger Americans," Larry pointed out gently.

"Is it not worth this to have security all of your life?" Phillipe demanded. "It astonishes me that in a country with such immense richness you do not have in the United States the social welfare programs that we take for granted in Europe. Even in Canada there is socialized medicine. In London, on a holiday, I fell and broke my arm. I went to a hos-

114

pital. My arm was X-rayed and set at no cost to me except for twenty pence for a pain killer."

The phone rang inside. Larry jumped up immediately, gesturing to Phillipe to sit.

"I'll get it. And I'll bring out more coffee," he tossed over one shoulder. "Phillipe always keeps a second percolator going."

"Did Lisette expect you to believe that Michel—who has been dead six years—pushed her down the stairs?" Phillipe shot at me the moment Larry was out of hearing. I sensed he knew Larry would disapprove of this questioning.

"I—I don't know." I stared at him defensively. "She plays this game that Michel is still alive—"

"But she is far too bright not to separate fact from fantasy. Could it be that she *knows* who pushed her down the stairs, and emotionally she is not able to accept it? Surely the lights were on in the corridor. On the stairs—"

"She was shoved, Phillipe. I doubt that she had an opportunity to turn around and look." Suddenly I felt a staggering hostility towards Phillipe. "And once everybody has gone to their rooms for the night, Henri turns out all the lights except for a pair of wall sconces. One on the stairs, one in the upstairs hall."

"But she said that Michel pushed her," Phillipe stubbornly repeated, "because she was running away from the truth."

"You're the child psychologist," I replied with an effort at humor. "You figure it out, Phillipe."

Larry came out whistling, with a fresh percolator of coffee.

"That was Monsieur Laval, Phillipe. We're both invited for dinner tonight." Larry glowed with approval.

"Claudine's cooking we never turn down." Phillipe held out his cup for Larry to refill. "We will be there." His eyes were serious, despite the levity in his voice. Whom did Phillipe suspect Lisette was protecting? "Now, another suggestion. Why don't the three of us drive up to Lausanne for lunch? You haven't yet seen Lausanne, have you, Andrea?"

"No. It sounds like fun." Lausanne was a university town, I recalled, with an international flavor.

Larry frowned slightly, though he nodded in agreement.

He would have preferred to drive to Lausanne with me without Phillipe, I decided with pleasure.

Instinct told me that Phillipe, despite this charming interest he was now displaying in me, was digging for information. He had an insatiable curiosity about what was happening at the chateau.

An hour later, after I had returned to the chateau to change quickly into something more suitable for lunch in Lausanne and to report my absence, the three of us climbed into the Fiat. Phillipe at the wheel, Larry and I in the rear. Today Phillipe was full of questions about the United States.

"For Christmas I'm buying him a set of travel books," Larry joked. "So the United States won't come as too much of a shock to him when he finally gets there."

"In the States I am buying a secondhand camper," Phillipe said with relish, "and I will tour the big cities and the small towns from the Atlantic to the Pacific. I will talk to people everywhere. Particularly children and teenagers. And I will come up with another book."

"Lisette was entranced with New York," Larry reminisced, "but I think American television made the greatest impression on her. She remembers every program she saw during the ten days she was there, and there were many!"

"Phillipe—" Suddenly I was serious. "The night she fell down the stairs—" I flinched before the use of the word because neither Phillipe, Larry, nor I believed she had fallen down that staircase. "Do you suppose she was awake because she'd had a nightmare? Because of the intruder in her room?" I was trying to fit pieces together in my mind.

Phillipe didn't speak for a moment.

"Lisette is a highly imaginative child. I would be amazed if she did not have some such repercussion from the intrusion in her room."

"Then if she was awakened suddenly from a nightmare, ran from her room in alarm—perhaps not fully awake yet —couldn't she have fallen?" I probed. "Are we all overly suspicious in believing she was shoved down the stairs? Just because she said Michel pushed her? That could be part of the nightmare!"

"You're trying to center these attacks on you," Phillipe

analyzed. "So that you can be less apprehensive about Lisette."

"Andrea, you can't wash away the intruder in Lisette's room," Larry pointed out. "He *knows* which is your room —he couldn't have made a mistake. And I can't believe there are two of them at work."

"I know. I'm just so angry at Lisette's being involved in this. It was terrifying enough," I admitted unwarily, "when it was only me."

"No more of this talk," Phillipe decided. "We are going into Lausanne. It is a beautiful city, though you need the build of a mountain goat if you try to get about much on foot. We will drive," he decreed with a grin, "have lunch at a terrace café that Larry and I are especially fond of, and then walk around a bit."

The drive to Lausanne was beautiful. But today, despite my determination to enjoy this excursion, I found it difficult to relax.

Lausanne, built on hills, was as beautiful as Phillipe had promised. A modern, cosmopolitan city, with elegant shops, attractive buildings, and high-rise apartments. Phillipe, who obviously had a running romance with the city, pointed out important landmarks. I tried to become involved.

We had lunch at the café, where the food matched the scenery. The streets were filled with tourists and with students attending summer courses at the local schools.

"Another day," Larry suggested, "we must take the boat from here to Villeneuve and visit the Castle of Chillon. Byron's Chillon," he smiled. "Byron carved his own name high on the stone pillar to which Bonnivard—the prisoner of Chillon—was chained. You can see it there today."

We walked a while after luncheon along the Avenue de la Gare inspecting the jewelry shop windows, the antique shops, admiring a particularly attractive office building. Walking towards the railway station, similar to the one in Geneva, Phillipe insisted we stop to have coffee at a sandwich bar where the coffee was ground to order.

"You cannot come to Lausanne without drinking this coffee," Phillipe rhapsodized. "And while we wait, you can inspect the entrance to the shortest subway in the world." He pointed to the sign above a booth next door. "The entire ride takes about six minutes."

117

Our coffee arrived. We drank with relish the best cup of coffee I'd ever had, I conceded.

"Before we head back for home we will detour to Ouchy," Phillipe decided. "The beach there is beautiful."

We drove slowly along the beach, tourist-mobbed at this time of year. Small sailboats were in abundance offshore.

"Andrea," Phillipe said with deceptive casualness, "Lisette's mother and brother died by drowning, did they not?" His eyes contemplative. Compassionate.

"Yes." All at once my throat was tight. Why must Phillipe obsessively return to the chateau this way? I didn't want to think about that tragic accident. I made a point now of not looking at the painting of Michel that hung in the hall at the chateau because it was painful to realize that I could never know this young brother. My only brother.

"How did it happen?"

With reluctance I told Phillipe about the accident. About Henri's being drunk for three days afterwards. What did Phillipe expect to discover by going back this way? It was morbid.

"Phillipe, are you looking for some connection between that accident and what's happening now?" Larry was skeptical.

"It appeared to be an accident," Phillipe emphasized. "Why was the red flag not on the boat?"

"Perhaps it wasn't tied properly," Larry suggested. "There could have been a sharp wind the night before." He squinted in thought. "A small child playing alone along the dock might have been attracted by the red scrap of cloth, pulled it off."

"There was a police investigation." I forced myself to mention this. Grandmère had been terribly upset, Dad said.

"The police would have investigated any accident," Larry said.

"Lisette's mother and brother died in that boat," Phillipe said slowly. "How did it happen that Lisette was not in the boat with them?"

"Lisette was in bed with a cold that day. She wasn't allowed out of her room." I sat tense on the rear seat leaning forward slightly to listen to Phillipe.

"So perhaps Lisette, too, was expected to be in that boat. And now someone wishes both Lisette and Andrea dead,"

Phillipe assessed. "Wishes everyone close to Armand Laval dead."

But none of us could come up with a name. Because we had not one shred of evidence that could be presented in a court. Not yet.

* * *

When I returned to the chateau, I found Lisette on a chaise beside the pool with Heidi stationed beside her.

"Why are Larry and Phillipe not with you?" she demanded as I approached. "They are to come to dinner." She was delighted at the prospect of a party.

"They'll be over later," I promised, dropping into a chair beside her, and scrutinizing her anxiously. "Shouldn't you be resting if you're going to be up late tonight?"

"I am resting," she chirped. "I've been resting out here all afternoon. I looked for you, but you were gone."

"We went into Lausanne for lunch," I explained, feeling guilty that I had not been there when Lisette looked for me.

"Are you truly going back to the States at the end of the month?" Her eyes were poignantly wistful.

"I think so," I edged. This newly found young sister had become incredibly dear. "I have a job at the UN."

"I think you will stay longer," Lisette said with an impish smile. "And when I come home on holidays we will see each other. Oh, that would be fun, Andrea!"

"We'll talk about it later," I promised.

"Here comes Pat," Lisette discovered with surprise. She was disappointed. She was enjoying this little *tête-a-tête* with me.

"Good afternoon," Pat said crisply, dropping into a chaise beside Lisette. She was carrying a small, wooden box and a scrap of sandpaper. "Lisette, I have only to finish the last bit of sandpapering, and I will be ready to do the design on your jewelry box." Pat was fumbling in her pocket of her slacks for a sheet of paper. "You must decide now which design you prefer."

I sat painfully tense while Lisette and Pat carried on absorbed conversation, marveling at Pat's show of deep affection for Lisette, when I suspected her of such macabre designs on both Lisette and myself. The jewelry box was ostensibly a labor of love.

I was relieved when Pat left us. I wished, painfully, that there was some way I could suggest to Dad that Lisette be supplied with a key so that her room could be locked at night. At least, let Heidi always sleep in Lisette's room.

Jeanne, leaving for the day, stopped at the pool to tell us that Grandmère insisted Lisette go to her room and take a brief nap before dinner. I noticed that Jeanne was wearing the pendant I had bought for her in Copenhagen.

"Come up to your room, too," Lisette cajoled. "Please, Andrea?" She turned with a mock frown to Heidi. "You, too, you naughty dog. She only wants to be with you, Andrea. She's forgetting all about me." Lisette leaned forward to throw her arms about Heidi's huge, shaggy head.

I went upstairs with Lisette, astonished to find that I, too, found the prospect of a brief nap inviting. But then, I'd been leading a full life since the day I arrived at Geneva Airport.

I slept no more than twenty minutes, yet felt considerably rested. Too early to go downstairs, I noted. Soak in a tub. Take time with my make-up. Tonight was a dinner party.

I wished, wistfully, that the slashed dress was intact. It was to have been my party dress. With Larry and Phillipe at dinner, tonight was definitely a special occasion.

I luxuriated in a warm, perfumed tub, debating about how to wear my hair. Up, I decided, sensing that this would please Grandmère. I sensed the wall between us would be soon obliterated and I would be fully accepted.

I'd wear the long, gaily printed skirt I'd bought for the planned Scandinavian trip with a long-sleeved white blouse. It would be festive with earrings and a necklace. Oh, let tonight be fun! All of us needed to relax from the tensions of the chateau.

I crossed to the window to pull the draperies tight. The night watchman was already on duty, though night had not completely fallen.

I pulled the draperies snugly across the balcony, at each of the windows. I left my room just as Lisette emerged from hers.

"You look just beautiful," she said, admiringly inspecting me. "I'm glad you wore a long skirt."

"I'm glad you did, too," I laughed. "You look adorable, Lisette."

She glowed.

"Grandmère didn't want me to have a long skirt," she confessed with a gamine smile. "But Dad came to visit me in Paris when he had business there, and I took him shopping."

"You are a canny one," I teased, leaning over to hug her. "Come, let's go down to our dinner party."

Reaching the foyer, we heard convivial voices in the library.

"Larry and Phillipe are here," Lisette said with a lively smile. "It's fun when we have company in the chateau, which isn't often because Grandmère becomes upset. I guess she thinks it's extra work for Claudine and Henri."

Hand in hand, Lisette and I sauntered down the hall. Pat was telling the others some old Scottish legend. She sounded in rare high spirits. Then Lisette and I entered the library, and she faltered in the midst of the story.

I forced a smile as I sat in a small, tapestry-covered chair beside Dad, conscious of the swift, approving smile Larry shot in my direction. Phillipe was being gallantly attentive to Pat. Grandmère had not yet come down.

Outside, the first signs of a summer storm were evident. Lightning zigzaged across the sky. Thunder rumbled. Through the open curtains I saw the blinking red lights on the opposite side of Lake Geneva, warning boats.

"A bad night for your watchman," Larry said compassionately, gazing out at the sky.

"Shall I have Henri tell him to take out the jeep?" Pat turned inquiringly to Dad. "He could sit there if it really begins to pour." Not in the chateau, I noted Pat's suggestion. In the jeep.

"Tell him if it rains, to take cover in the garage," Dad instructed. "He has a view of most of the grounds from there."

Pat went off to brief Henri. A moment later Grandmère arrived. A beautiful, elegant lady even in her seventies, I conceded with silent admiration. Tonight she had made a special effort to appear her best. The dress was surely a designer's original. Her jewelry was exquisite and expensive. But I saw the constraint in her smile, the tiredness in her eyes.

"I do hope the storm blows over." Grandmère flinched at a rumble of thunder. She loathed noise, I recalled.

"It will storm," Dad said gently, "but it will be over quickly."

Pat returned to tell us that Claudine was prepared to serve dinner. Phillipe, with a shy charm that Grandmère relished, offered her his arm. She truly liked Phillipe. I wasn't sure of her feelings towards Larry, though she respected his abilities as a tutor. Phillipe's Old World manners, pulled out on specific occasions, were more to her taste.

Lisette hung on to Dad. Pat and I followed with Larry, who was engrossed in a Scottish folk tale Pat was telling.

Phillipe and Dad became almost immediately involved in a political discussion about France. Until now I'd forgotten that Dad was French and that he had lived in Switzerland only since the tragedy. Grandmère and Pat were discussing Lisette's new school. Lisette, usually so vivacious, was quiet. At regular intervals I glanced at her with concern. Her eyes so stormy. Her mouth set into tight rebellion. Why was Dad letting Grandmère get away with this?

Lisette didn't want to go to school in London—surely that was clear to everyone in the chateau. Why couldn't she live at home and attend school in Geneva? Yet who was I to interfere? What power would I have with Dad if I tried, on something where Grandmère was so determined?

Lisette disliked Phillipe, I realized with a start, intercepting a look she shot in his direction. With that fine sensitivity of hers, she realized Phillipe didn't like her. So Lisette was spoiled. With reason! How could he hold this against her, I thought impatiently. A child psychologist should understand.

Claudine had prepared a sumptuous dinner. Tonight there was no ordinary pâté but pâté de foie gras. Carrot soup, roast leg of lamb with parsley potatoes and asparagus Milanaise, a tossed green salad. For dessert an elegantly molded ice cream bought at a *patisserie* in Nyon.

We all ate with gusto, retiring at Dad's suggestion to the

library for coffee. Grandmère was nervous, as she had been all through dinner, because the storm was in full force.

"The storm is lessening," Dad said gently, sensitive to Grandmère's unease. "It will be over in a few minutes."

"I wonder if Claudine thought to send a tray out to the watchman?" Grandmère rose to her feet. "I will go see to it myself."

She could have rung for Henri or Claudine, I thought. But she was restless and welcomed this opportunity to break away from the now politically oriented dinner party. The discussion held little interest for her.

"You're quiet tonight," Larry said softly. "Bushed?"

"A little," I admitted. "But having fun."

"You're looking beautiful." His eyes said much more, and my heart was suddenly thumping.

"Andrea—" Lisette left Dad to come to me. "I'm going out to ask Grandmère if I may have mint tea instead of hot chocolate. Sometimes she allows this. Would you like mint tea with me, instead of coffee? It's delicious," she said persuasively.

"I'd love it," I agreed, eager to please Lisette.

A few moments later Grandmère returned, trailed by Lisette, who importantly carried a tray with two cups of mint tea.

"I allow her to have tea only on special occasions," Grandmère explained conscientiously. "But I doubt that it will keep her awake tonight when she is remaining up far past her normal bedtime."

"Andrea is taking me into Geneva to have lunch at Perle du Lac," Lisette said lightly. But her eyes, fastened on Grandmère, were anticipating conflict. "Next week," Lisette added with an elfin smile in my direction, her eyes pleading for corroboration.

"If Grandmère approves," I interjected with diplomacy.

"We'll discuss it next week." Grandmère stated and turned to join the discussion between Dad and Phillipe.

As soon as Lisette had finished her tea, Grandmère insisted she go upstairs to bed.

"It is late enough," Grandmère said sternly. "You are becoming terribly spoiled."

Inadvertently I glanced at Phillipe, who felt so strongly

123

about this. He was gazing at Grandmère with an odd intensity. An almost terrifying reproach in his eyes.

"Lisette, to bed." Dad backed up Grandmère with a show of authority. Pat smiling indulgently at Lisette. "But first come say good night properly."

Not long after Grandmère and Lisette had gone up to their rooms, I began to yawn with disconcerting frequency.

"To bed with you, also, Andrea," Dad ordered, his eyes tender. "All this mountain air is making you sleepy." But I saw a seriousness in his eyes, also. He knew how tense I was after the incidents of this past week. The most alarming week of my life.

Irritated with myself, I said good night and left the three men and Pat to continue their dissection of the United Nations operation in Africa. Normally I would have enjoyed joining the discussion because Mr. Svedborg was active in this area, and I was intrigued by the reports he made after his various trips to Africa.

In my room I locked myself in as usual. I paused sleepily, to glance below at the sturdy night watchman who walked slowly about the grounds, now that the storm was over, with a revolver at his fingertips. But the danger lay here within the chateau, I knew.

I prepared for bed, knowing tonight I would have no difficulty in sleeping. The restless nights were catching up with me. What a shame I had not been wide awake enough to remain downstairs!

I fell asleep to the muted sounds of the voices from the library below, knowing it would be a while before the others decided to call it a night.

* * *

In my heavy slumber I was vaguely conscious of a telephone ringing somewhere. In the middle of the night, I thought groggily? And then I abandoned thinking. Tired. So terribly tired.

Some odd aroma in my room. What was it? Something acrid. Unpleasant. I should get up. Open a window. But I can't. I'm too tired. It'll go away. In a little while it'll go away. That awful, burning smell—

Chapter Twelve

Still enmeshed in sleep, annoyed at this intrusion, I was conscious of a dog whimpering close by. Pawing at a door. My door. Heidi, I decided in the small portion of my mind that was active. Now she was barking. What was the matter with her?

I burrowed my face in my pillow wanting to shut out the sound of the barking. Oh, why didn't Heidi shut up? She'd wake the whole house! Without opening my eyes I guessed that it was the middle of the night.

"Andrea!" Suddenly Dad's voice filtered through to me. Muffled. Anxious. "Andrea!" He was trying to open the door. Groggily I remembered that it was locked.

I made an effort to clear my head. To wake up. Aware of voices in the corridor. What was the matter? I forced my eyes open and was temporarily immobilized at what I saw.

Flames wrapped themselves about my desk, threatened to engulf the long, lush draperies at both windows on either side of it.

"Pat, wake Henri!" Dad ordered. "Maman, go to Lisette."

My door crashed open beneath the frenzy of Dad's onslaught. Simultaneously, I darted from the bed, reaching for my robe at its foot.

"Get out, Andrea!" Dad ordered.

"Heidi, stay!" Pat's voice, in the hall was sharp. "Monsieur Laval, shall I call for the firemen?"

"Not yet," Dad said. "Perhaps we can handle this without them. Get Henri!" he repeated.

"Claudine has gone for him."

Dad reached for a blanket, beat at the flames. Ignoring his order to leave the room, I raced into the bathroom, grabbed the lucite wastepaper basket, dumped a collection of tissues on the floor, and filled it with water.

"Let me have that!" Dad ordered tersely.

While Dad doused sections of the draperies on one side, I took the blanket and grappled with the flames that threatened to devour the draperies on the other side. Dad dashed into the bathroom to refill the wastebasket with water. I continued to beat at the burning draperies with the wool blanket.

"Mon Dieu!" Henri stared in shock for an instant from the doorway, then rushed into action knowing spare blankets were kept on a shelf in the closet.

Downstairs someone pounded on the door. The night watchman had seen the flames from outside.

"It's all right," Pat called down crisply. "The fire is under control. Please continue your patrol."

Henri tossed a blanket completely over the desk, muffling the flames that had destroyed the sheaf of magazines I had brought up to read. Dad refilled the wastebasket again. In moments the fire was completely out. The desk was a black, charred ruin. The remains of the draperies were sodden and useless.

Claudine and Pat huddled together at my door, white and tense. Pat held tightly to Heidi's collar, while the dog whimpered her anxiety.

"It's all right, Heidi," I soothed. "It's all right now."

"Claudine will prepare another room for you," Dad said tiredly, his eyes recoiling from the damage done by the brief blaze. "Claudine, I am sorry to bother you at this hour of the night," Dad said apologetically.

"Henri will help me," Claudine said briskly. "We will have a room ready in ten minutes. Henri, come."

"I'll make coffee," Pat said solicitously. "Are you all right?" Her eyes searched Dad's face.

"We are fine, Pat," Dad reassured her. "And coffee would be marvelous."

Pat went directly down to the kitchen. Dad reached to

squeeze my hand reassuringly for a moment, knowing I was trembling, now that the fire was out.

"Let us look in on Lisette before we go downstairs," he said gently.

Grandmère sat at the edge of the bed, watching Lisette, who was sound asleep. Grandmère's face was distraught. The hand that rested on Lisette's covers was visibly unsteady. Heidi, making faint sounds, settled herself beside Lisette's bed.

"Lisette heard nothing." Despite her distress, Grandmère kept her voice even. "But I will sit with her awhile."

"Pat's making coffee," I said gently. "Would you like me to bring you a cup when it's ready?"

Grandmère smiled. For the first time I felt complete communication with her.

"Thank you, no, Andrea. I will sit here for a few minutes, and then I will go back to bed."

Dad and I went downstairs, settled ourselves in the library. Lights were everywhere in the chateau now, it seemed. We could hear Pat out in the kitchen.

"I cannot imagine how that fire started," Dad said with frustration. "How could it possibly have happened?" His eyes rested uneasily on me. "Your door was locked—" Meaning, nobody could have entered to start the fire.

"I bought a key," I admitted, ashamed that I had not been honest with Dad about this. "Which was silly," I conceded with an effort at humor, "because it's just one of those passkeys you buy at any hardware store. But I—I felt safer with the door locked." But somehow a fire was started in my room.

"Your windows were locked, Andrea?" His voice was exasperated.

"Yes." And a watchman was prowling about the grounds.

"Then there's only one answer. This fire was just a freakish accident." Dad was trying to sound convinced. But neither of us accepted this explanation.

We both started at the sound of voices about the grounds.

"We are neighbors," I heard Phillipe explain loudly in French to the watchman on the grounds. "We saw all the lights go on in the chateau. We were concerned."

"There was a fire," the watchman explained importantly. "It is all over."

Dad crossed to a window, opened it, threw the shutters wide.

"It is all right," Dad called out to the watchman. "Phillipe, come around to the front door."

Dad strode down the hall to open the door, while I waited. Phillipe and Larry walked inside.

"I woke up and I could not go back to sleep," Phillipe explained. "I got out of bed for a book to read because sometimes that helps me get back to sleep. I saw the lights go on—I knew something must be wrong. I immediately woke Larry so that we could come over and help."

"The watchman said there was a fire," Larry said guardedly. And then I saw the relief wash over his face when he spied me in the corridor.

"Nobody was hurt," Dad reassured him. "The fire was in Andrea's room." He paused to lock the door. "Come into the library. Pat is making coffee for us."

Dad gave Larry and Phillipe a succinct rundown on the fire. Both listened intently. Larry grinned as Dad reported my participation in putting out the fire.

"You have no idea how it started?" Phillipe frowned in concentration.

"I cannot figure it out." Dad pantomimed his incomprehension. "Andrea's door was locked. The windows were locked. The watchman was on duty outside. No one—no one," Dad emphasized, "could have entered the room. The fire could not have been engineered earlier. Any kind of timing device would involve an explosion. There was none."

"Let's go back and dissect it slowly," Larry suggested. "Now, first of all, Heidi's barking woke up the household?"

"Yes. I woke up to hear Heidi barking and scratching at a door," Dad said. "I hurried out into the hall to discover her very upset at Andrea's door."

"Doesn't she usually stay in Lisette's room?" Larry asked.

"Lisette is trying to break her of the habit of jumping up onto the foot of her bed," Dad explained. "When Heidi does this, Lisette puts her out into the hall for the night."

"Thank heavens, she did tonight!" I shuddered in recall. "I was sleeping as though I'd been drugged—" I stopped short, aware of the reaction my words had evoked in the others. Had I been drugged? Lisette, too, was sleeping heavily. Had we both been drugged?

"What do you remember, Andrea?" Larry probed.

"I—I was sleeping heavily." I fought to sound matter-of-fact. The pleasing aroma of fresh coffee perking in the kitchen was strangely reassuring.

"Go on, Andrea," Larry urged. "Recreate the whole scene in your mind, bit by bit."

"I was sleeping heavily," I repeated, squinting in my effort to reconstruct those few minutes before Dad burst into my room. "I thought I heard a phone ringing. Then I heard Heidi whimpering outside my door. She began to bark. She sounded terribly upset—"

"A phone ringing where?" Larry leaned forward intently. Dad and Phillipe watched him closely, knowing he was in pursuit of a clue, yet unable to follow him thus far. "Ringing where, Andrea?"

"Somewhere in the chateau." I hesitated. "It could have been in my room."

"That's how the fire started!" Larry rose to his feet in excitement. The rest of us stared at him in incomprehension.

"What do you mean, Larry?" My heart was suddenly pounding.

"My father was an insurance investigator. I grew up hearing about all the methods of committing arson. A favored way—because it puts the aronist away from the scene —is to start a fire by using a telephone."

"I do not understand." Dad gazed at Larry in bewilderment.

"A pad of matches and a piece of sandpaper are rigged into the phone mechanism. It's amazingly simple, once you see how it's done. Remove a few screws, insert the pad of matches and sandpaper. Then go away, make the phone call from a distance at any chosen time. In this case, in the middle of the night, when everyone would presumably be asleep."

"What happens?" Phillipe demanded. "I do not understand the mechanics of this."

"The friction of the phone ringing causes the matches to hit the sandpaper and ignite. Andrea was sleeping heavily. She wasn't aware of the fire until Heidi began to bark. It was lucky that Heidi was in the hall, rather than in Lisette's room!" Larry's eyes rested seriously on me.

"But the phone that rang in my room rang in other rooms, too, didn't it? I mean, it was an extension—" I was fumbling. My mind was in disorder at this point.

"The main line is there." Dad pointed to the phone on the library desk. "You have an extension in your room, and Maman has one. There are no others."

Didn't Grandmère hear the phone? I pondered this only fleetingly because Phillipe brought up another point.

"How could anyone have called from this phone to Andrea's?" Phillipe questioned. "He would get only a busy signal. There would be no ring."

"There is another line in my office," Dad explained. "Anyone could go in there to call." He sighed heavily. "Monday morning I am scheduled to go into Geneva to my office. My first task will be to consult a firm of private investigators. This cannot go on. We must know who is doing these terrible things."

"Andrea, will you please serve the gentlemen their coffee?" We all turned to face Pat, who stood in the doorway. Her knuckles were white as she clutched the tray. Her face strained. Walking down the hall, she must have heard the bit about the sandpaper. She knew I remembered her using the sandpaper on Lisette's jewelry box. "I'll go back for extra cups for us."

"Thank you, Pat." I forced a smile as I took the tray, carried it to a table.

I waited until I was sure Pat was back in the kitchen before I spoke again. My voice low.

"Both Lisette and I must have been drugged." I tried to keep my hand steady as I poured coffee. "Lisette would surely have heard Heidi barking. So would I."

"When were you drugged?" Larry picked up quickly. "At dinner?" He frowned. "Just Lisette and you?"

"After dinner," I said, "Lisette and I had mint tea. Everybody else had coffee."

Grandmère had been out in the kitchen, talking with Claudine about a tray for the watchman, when Lisette went out to ask that we have mint tea. Even so, somebody in that kitchen managed to slip sleeping pills—or some similar drug—into our mint tea. That was the only way it could have happened.

Where was Pat, I asked myself? I couldn't recall her leaving the library from the time we entered until I went up to my room.

"Andrea—" Phillipe's voice was urgent. "Who was in the kitchen while the tea was being made?"

"No, I cannot believe that Andrea and Lisette were drugged," Dad intervened, visibly upset at this accusation. "We must not probe this way. I will talk with the investigators on Monday. They will ask questions. They will discover who is responsible for these terrible things."

* * *

"We should get home," Phillipe said gently when he had finished his coffee, his eyes in communication with Larry. Dad was withdrawn now, absently pouring himself another cup of coffee. "I am glad that no one was hurt in the fire."

"For this we can thank Heidi." Dad's eyes rested painfully on me then moved onto Phillip and Larry. "Thank you for coming over this way in the middle of the night. It is good to have neighbors who have such concern for our welfare."

I walked with Larry and Phillipe to the door conscious of Larry's anxiety for my safety, knowing the questions that plagued at him. Who had called me in the middle of the night, to trigger that fire? There were no doubts in the minds of any of us that this was how the fire was set. The phone call which had not disturbed Grandmère. Or had she picked it up in her room to discover the caller gone? Tomorrow I must ask about this.

"Sleep late if you can," Larry urged. "Then let me pick you up for a drive. We'll have brunch somewhere along the road." Unexpectedly he grinned. "Phillipe's going to be working all day tomorrow. He already told me."

"I could push it off for a day," Phillipe warned with a glint of humor.

"You do and there'll be a case of murder here—" Larry flinched, shook his head in self-reproach. "Work, Phillipe," he said sternly, and turned to me again. "I'll pick you up around noon, Andrea. All right?"

"That'll be great." I didn't honestly expect to sleep. The drug had worn off. The coffee would hardly be a sleep inducer. And I was terribly tense, but I cherished the prospect of spending a part of the day away from the chateau. Away from fear. With Larry.

I closed and locked the door behind Larry and Phillipe, hearing them talking casually with the night watchman. Dad was coming down the hall now. Pat, I surmised, was taking care of the dishes in the kitchen, rather than leave them overnight for Claudine.

Henri stood at the head of the stairs as I turned from the door.

"Mademoiselle, your room is ready," he said, his voice devoid of emotion. "The guest room just beyond Monsieur Laval's."

"Thank you, Henri."

"Monsieur Laval—" Henri leaned forward over the bannister to talk to Dad. "I have opened the shutters and windows in the room where the fire took place to clear the air. Is that all right?"

"Yes, thank you, Henri," Dad approved. "Monday we will arrange for the repairs."

"Bon soir, Mademoiselle, Monsieur," Henri said stiffly, and moved out of view. Actually, it was morning already. In another hour dawn would be seen above the Alps across the lake.

"Andrea, you will be all right tonight." Dad reached for my hand, sighing tiredly. "I cannot understand all this. Who wishes to hurt me this way? To harm what is dearest to me in life!"

Still, I thought, Dad refused to accept the fact that someone within the chateau—someone he knew—was responsible. Because everyone within the chateau was close to him. Except for Jeanne, who came in from the village by the day. Jeanne, who had remained late tonight to help with the dinner party.

Jeanne had been in the kitchen when Lisette went out to ask Grandmère about the mint tea. A coldness crept over me as I reconstructed this in my mind. Jeanne desperately wanted to be rich. To her I was a jet-age Cinderella. She looked at me with such envy.

No! Not Jeanne, I rejected the thought. Envious of my position here at the chateau, yes. But, no, Jeanne would not stoop to murder!

Would she?

Chapter Thirteen

Dad walked me to my new room and opened the door. A light had been left on in welcome. I stared inside, forcing a show of interest. A charming room, as I had expected, decorated in sprightly blues and greens. The geometrically designed draperies drawn tight. The bed was turned down invitingly. But right now I was hardly concerned with the attractiveness of my surroundings.

"Try to sleep, Andrea," Dad soothed. "You will be all right. Nothing else will happen tonight." But despite the confidence in his voice, his eyes were troubled. "Soon—very soon—this nightmare will be over."

"Good night, Dad." I leaned forward to kiss him. Poor Dad. So upset for me. "And stop worrying."

Dad went down the hall to his own room. I shut my door and stood there with uncertainty because I realized the door must remain unlocked. But Dad was right, I tried to shore up my courage. Whoever set the fire in my bedroom was unlikely to try again tonight. Instinct told me there would be another attempt. A more desperate one because failure must be eating away at whoever plotted my death.

Knowing the door must remain unlocked, for lack of a key, I couldn't restrain myself from setting a chair beneath the knob, even while I jeered at myself for this puny attempt at safety. But if anyone tried to come in, I would waken immediately.

Those guns in the case in the library. I should have a loaded gun beside my bed. But no, I could never bring myself to shoot, to take a life, even with a gun in my hand. Not even in self-defense.

I took off my robe, slid beneath the covers, pulled them snugly about my shoulders against the night chill, wishing, wistfully, that Heidi was here at the foot of my bed with that sonorous bark to warn off intruders. But Heidi must watch over Lisette. Poor baby, I thought with tenderness, sleeping so soundly because of that drug in her tea.

I closed my eyes, determined to fall asleep again, trying to forget the horror of my awaking in the other room, to the blaze that enveloped my desk and traveled up the curtains.

Eventually, from simple exhaustion, I fell asleep.

* * *

I came awake with a start. The memory of last night instantly rolled over me with fresh alarm. I pulled myself into a sitting position, struggling to clear my mind. What time was it? In the unfamiliar room I sought a clock.

A green marble clock sat on a wall bracket opposite my bed, between a pair of windows. Just past eleven. I threw aside the covers with sudden urgency, although I had almost an hour before Larry would come for me.

In my robe and slippers I walked down the hall to my old room. At the door I hesitated briefly gearing myself to enter. But Henri had been here earlier, I discovered.

The charred desk had been removed and the draperies taken down. The carpeting between the windows was sodden with water, stained. The wallpaper charred, the ceiling dark from smoke. The acrid scent of a recent blaze was still in the room. I suppressed a shudder. I wasn't likely to return to this room during my visit. I wouldn't want to sleep here again.

I collected what I planned to wear for the day, started to my new room to wash and dress. Later, when I returned from the drive with Larry, I would move everything completely.

Involuntarily I slowed down at Dad's door, hearing the muted sound of Grandmère's voice as she talked inside with Dad. Was she urging Dad to send me home? Instantly, I felt guilty that I had suspected this.

I dressed quickly, with an eye on the clock. I was impa-

135

tient to be with Larry in the Fiat, to leave the chateau behind for a few hours. When I passed Dad's door again, there was only silence.

Downstairs Lisette was practicing at the piano. How talented she was! And Michel? Had he been as gifted as Lisette? Poor Michel, who lived hardly long enough to display his gifts. I felt a poignant sense of loss for the small brother I had never known.

"Good morning." I forced a light tone as I looked in on Lisette. "How're you feeling this morning?"

"I'm fine." Lisette removed her hands from the piano. Her small face was anxious. "Did I wake you? Father said I was not to practice before eleven because you would sleep late. It *is* eleven, isn't it?"

"Darling, yes," I soothed. "Go on and practice. I'm going out to the kitchen to ask Claudine for coffee."

"Father said there was a fire in your room last night," Lisette pursued, wide-eyed. "He said Heidi woke him up so that he was able to go to you before—" She hesitated, flinching from ugliness, "before you could get hurt."

"That's right, Lisette. Heidi's a heroine." I tried to make last night sound like an adventure.

"I'm so glad I put Heidi out. She keeps jumping up on the bed and she's shedding so badly. It makes my nose itch when Heidi's hair is all over the bed." Lisette smiled appealingly. "I'm glad Heidi woke Father."

I left Lisette and walked down the hall, turning in towards the kitchen. Claudine and Pat stood together next to the window in absorbed, low-pitched conversation.

"Excuse me," I said casually. Claudine and Pat started. Color flooded Pat's face as she turned to me. What had Claudine and Pat been discussing that my arrival so disconcerted them? "May I have some coffee, Claudine?"

"It will be ready in a moment," Claudine said with an air of self-consciousness, which, I was certain, had nothing to do with her reluctance to speak English. "I will bring it to you on the terrace, Mademoiselle." She hesitated. Surprisingly, she seemed less belligerent this morning. "It is a beautiful day. You will enjoy the view."

"Thank you, Claudine." I smiled and spun away from them knowing Pat was waiting for me to leave to resume the conversation I had interrupted.

136

I sat at the table on the terrace to wait for my coffee, my shoulder bag and jacket on a chair beside me, in readiness for my jaunt with Larry. It was an exquisite day. Dozens of boats were out on the lake.

In the distance I heard church bells, and visualized the parade of villagers in their Sunday finery. From Phillipe's house came the sound of a typewriter. Phillipe was obviously working as scheduled.

Claudine came out onto the terrace in a few moments with hot croissants and a carafe of fragrant coffee. I reached for a flaky croissant with an awareness of my hunger. Just one, I cautioned myself. I was having brunch with Larry.

Sitting here on the terrace, gazing down at Lake Geneva as I ate and sipped Claudine's excellent coffee, I felt as though last night was a million years behind me. Another life.

Yet I could not completely relax. Deep within me beat an insistent warning. Fresh danger lay ahead. Someone in the chateau was growing desperate, determined to hurt—to *kill* me.

Lisette continued to practice. For this I was grateful. Her fingers on the piano keys was an oddly reassuring sound. Then my attention turned to the view directly below. Someone was emerging from the house. With the sunlight in my eyes it was difficult to see if it was Larry or Phillipe. No, it must be Larry. I could hear Phillipe at the typewriter. My heart pounded in anticipation. Larry had become very special to me.

I watched the Fiat move out of the driveway onto the road, drive down the hundred feet or so to the steep incline that led up to the chateau. I finished my coffee, left the table to walk towards the driveway, purse swinging from my shoulder, coat hanging over one arm.

"You look chipper," Larry called out, leaning over to open the car door for me.

"I didn't expect to sleep at all," I acknowledged, sliding onto the seat beside Larry. Was it possible I'd known him only a week? "But when I dropped off, I didn't wake until eleven."

"What do you say to brunch cafeteria style, when we get around to it?" Larry suggested while we headed down the

137

driveway, his eyes bright with laughter. "Not quite Perle du Lac."

"What's wrong with cafeterias?" I tossed back, relaxing now that we were leaving the chateau behind us.

"There are some hardy souls that walk up there from here" Larry chuckled reminiscently. "The natives tell you casually, 'Oh, it's just up there—' " He nodded to a lookout point seemingly not far above. "Phillipe and I tried it just once. It was like scaling the Matterhorn. The next time we took the car."

"What is it?" I peered curiously in the direction Larry indicated.

"Signal de Bougy. It's a public recreation center, with a cafeteria and a small store for take-out foods and souvenirs. You can picnic if you like—there're spots for grilling franks or steaks. Here's where the Swiss from the towns around here come for a day's outing."

"Sounds great." I knew Larry was being deliberately casual, to take my mind off what happened last night. I guessed, too, that Phillipe and he had discussed this in depth before they went to bed last night—and I was anxious to know their conclusions. But I wouldn't let myself ask questions, I promised silently. This was a period of relaxation. And I would just enjoy being with Larry.

We drove into the village, swung around sharply right at the sign that pointed to Signal de Bougy and drove steadily upward. I could understand why Larry preferred to take the car.

On the top we found parking space, left the car to walk to an observation point.

"Isn't this sensational?" Larry scanned the scenery with appreciation.

"Yes." My gaze followed his. "But it's also sensational from the chateau." Still, I viewed the splendor of the Alps with awe.

"There's the chateau." Larry dropped an arm about my waist, prodded me towards the protective fencing. "Right down there." He pointed slightly to our left, below.

Together, we gazed down at the chateau. The pool was dramatically blue and the terrace sunlit, host now only to Heidi, who sprawled there asleep. And I—I was exquisitely aware of Larry's arm about my waist. Aware of his nearness. We might have passed each other a dozen times in New York, but we had to come to a chateau forty kilometers from Geneva to meet.

"Let's walk," Larry commanded. "Isn't it beautiful up here?"

Our eyes swept pleasurably over the vast, immaculately maintained acreage. Benches were set at strategic intervals among colorful flower beds. Signs diplomatically warned picnickers to keep off the grass in certain areas, to be neat.

Larry and I paused to read a sign:

"La Liberté De L'Homme Reside Dans L'Acceptation De Son Devoir." (G. Duttweiler) *"Au Signal De Bougy Vous Etes Libres! Et Vous Avez Des Devoirs. Respecter La Liberté De Votre Prochain: Admirer Les Animaux Sans Les Nourrir; Protéger La Nature. Nous Vous Faisons Confidance."*

"Now how could anyone mess up this delightful place in the face of that?" I said flippantly. For this little while I felt myself just another American tourist, out with someone special, framing words in my mind to tell Kathy and Betty Lynne about Larry. Kathy the romantic would be enthralled with our meeting this way. Betty Lynne, always faintly suspicious of someone new, was reluctant to jump headlong into a romantic attachment—as I was eager to do in this instance.

We sat on a bench, talking awhile about New York, feeling a pleasant nostalgia, and avoiding any conversation about the chateau because last night was too painfully sharp in our minds.

I might have died in that fire, but for Heidi and Dad. At irregular intervals, despite my efforts to erase the scene from my mind, I remembered opening my eyes to the blaze in my room. The desk, the draperies, in flames. Remembered the panic which inundated me for a sickening few seconds. How many times could luck be on my side?

We left the bench to walk casually along the paths. Holding hands. Feeling such satisfaction at being alone together. Larry was now talking about his childhood in Connecticut. We might have been any romantic young couple spending a Sunday in the park.

"Feel ready for brunch?" Larry asked. "If we wait much later, the cafeteria will be mobbed."

"I'm ready." I smiled.

We walked back towards the sprawling cafeteria. Families occupied every outdoor table, some with picnic baskets providing the main courses, with desserts and beverages purchased at the cafeteria.

"We'll have to eat inside," Larry said with a rueful smile. "I forgot the place was so crowded on weekends."

"I don't mind," I said quickly, sniffing the savory aromas that emerged as we approached.

Inside we inadvertently lined up at what proved to be the dessert and sandwich section.

"Chaud voilà," a rotund, good-humored woman ahead of us turned around to explain. She pointed to a counter around the bend from where we stood in line, her eyes saying she approved of Larry and me as a couple. Was my face a giveaway, I wondered? Did she know how deeply I was attracted to Larry?

Laughing at our ignorance, Larry and I scurried to join the proper line and read the menus with vocal appreciation of the prices.

"Everything smells so marvelous," I said enthusiastically, watching the parade of plates pass from the counterwoman to the patrons.

"What about Eggs à la Russe for an exotic brunch?" Larry viewed the steam table with interest. "Or the veal and noodles. At four francs!" he chortled, with a tourist's delight at acquiring a bargain.

We made our way with our trays to a table by the window. The cafeteria reverberated with voices speaking French, German, Italian. Larry returned for our coffee, acquired from a gadget similar to the American Automat dispensers, except that here—as at the stand in Lausanne—the beans were ground and the coffee made right at the counter.

We ate with relish, and Larry returned for second cups of coffee and some flaky pastries. No bus boys here, we noted with amusement. Instead, patrons were exhorted to stack their trays after dining and deposit on the racks of the "chariots" provided for this purpose.

We lingered at our table and it was pleasant to sit and listen to the holiday conversation on all sides. In this anonymity I felt safe.

140

At the small store attached to the cafeteria I bought a collection of postcards for Lisette. I reminding myself that next week I must take her into Geneva for lunch, as I'd promised. It would be good for Lisette, too, to be away from the chateau for a day.

On the way back to the parking lot we came face to face with Jeanne and a young man. They were arguing bitterly, oblivious of us at first. Then Jeanne spied me and stopped dead. Her face flooded with color and her eyes were angry as she forced a greeting.

"*Bonjour, Mademoiselle, Monsieur.*"

"*Bonjour,* Jeannie," I said softly, but Jeanne and her friend had already moved past us.

"Now you know how Jeanne spends her day off." Larry sounded amused, but his eyes were speculative. "Though she was hardly in a good mood."

"She's going away to college in the fall. Did you know?" I was suddenly uncomfortable about Jeanne's anger. I'd seen, too, her swift, stealthy glance at Larry as she swept past me. She was comparing her companion to Larry. The comparison seemed unfavorable to her escort.

Jeanne was frantically ambitious for the material things of life. She was envious of me for what she felt I'd attained. I'd been upset to discover this earlier. *How envious?*

As we were driving back to the chateau, Larry brought up the subject of the death of Michel and his mother.

"Phillipe keeps getting signals in his mind that link their deaths to these attempts on your life and Lisette's," he explained uneasily. "Phillipe thinks we're walking right over one chunk of information that's the whole key."

"If you're thinking of Pat, no." I shook my head with conviction. "Pat couldn't have drugged Lisette and me last night. I went over the whole evening in my mind, second by second. Pat didn't leave the library from the time Lisette went out to ask about the mint tea until Lisette and I both went to our rooms. She stayed there with Dad and Phillipe and you."

"On the strength of that you want to rule out Pat?" Larry was skeptical.

"Larry, she couldn't have drugged us," I said flatly. "That removes her from suspicion, to me."

"How do you tie Jeanne into this?" Larry's question

brought me up sharply. "Something bothers you about Jeanne."

"I'm suspicious of everybody," I hedged. "She—she was working late last night, to help with the dinner. She was in the kitchen, Larry."

"But she couldn't have been involved with Michel's death. That happened in France."

"I keep wondering, too, if there could be some connection. But there's so little to go on!"

"Your father's private investigators will grill everybody in the chateau," Larry warned, and smiled faintly. "Perhaps even Phillipe and me. Claudine and Henri will be dreadfully upset."

"I know." I recoiled from the vision of Grandmère being put through that kind of ordeal. But the investigators would insist on a free rein. In their eyes, I realized, even Dad was suspect. "Larry," I said curiously, "do you suppose these attacks on Lisette would have happened if I hadn't arrived? Am I the catalyst?"

"I think so, Andrea." His eyes left the wheel for a moment to rest on me. "Of course, we can't know. I wish you'd take Lisette and go to stay at the Geneva apartment for a few days. Until the investigators come up with something. Your father would feel better if you did."

"I'll discuss it with Dad tomorrow." I promised reluctantly, knowing the chateau spelled danger for me.

"I'll drive in and take Lisette and you to Perle du Lac for lunch if you move into the apartment," Larry promised.

We drove through the Sunday-empty village towards the chateau. The vines were heavy with grapes, though Larry told me picking was still weeks distant. Approaching Larry's house, we heard the clicking of the typewriter. Phillipe was still at work.

Dad and Lisette lay on chaises beside the pool, drying their swim suits in the sun. Dad waved to us as we pulled up into the driveway. Lisette darted forward to greet us. At the same moment Grandmère leaned from an upstairs window, waved to Larry and me, called to Lisette.

"Lisette, come upstairs and get out of that wet suit before you catch cold. Immediately, young lady."

I hugged Lisette exuberantly, despite her wet suit, and prodded her on into the chateau.

"Grandmère will insist I go into a tub," Lisette said resignedly. "I'll see you later. Bye, Larry." She shot him a whimsical smile before she ran to the door.

Dad beckoned to us to join him, thrusting aside the pile of newspapers he'd been perusing.

"Andrea, tell Claudine to send out coffee for us," Dad ordered. "Larry, sit down and talk to me."

"Dad, put on a robe," I coaxed. "The sun's going down."

"Just like her grandmother," Dad chuckled. "Won't let a man think for himself." But he was reaching for his robe as I strode towards the kitchen.

Neither Claudine nor Henri were in sight. I went about putting up the coffee myself. I brought down china and a tray as I waited for the coffee to perk, dug out silver. For the first time, I realized, I felt as though I belonged in the chateau, that it was my home.

I glanced out the kitchen window. Henri was bringing the Bentley out of the garage. To wash it, I guessed. Claudine must be up in her room napping until it was time to prepare dinner. Jeanne, of course, was off on Sunday. There was, right now, a deceptive peacefulness about the chateau.

When the coffee had perked, I poured it into a carafe, set it on a tray with the china, and carried it along the pebbled path to the poolside sitting area. Dad and Larry were in earnest conversation, their faces serious. As I approached they stopped talking. Larry came forward to take the tray from me. What had they been talking about so earnestly?

"So now I will see what kind of coffee you make," Dad joked. "If it is bad, we will send you back to America." Suddenly his face was sober. "I hope you will stay here, Andrea. Indefinitely."

"I—I think I'd like to," I said involuntarily. I saw Dad's face light up at this admission. Larry, too, seemed delighted. "Let's talk about it next week."

But how could I talk about staying indefinitely when somebody was trying to kill me? Even while Larry urged me to remain in Switzerland, he'd specifically said, "go into Geneva to the apartment." Away from the chateau.

How did we know that whoever was after Lisette and me would not follow us to the apartment? Yet I couldn't bear the prospect of leaving Switzerland and leaving my newly

143

found family. I wanted to stay! Realistically, I knew I should run.

What about taking Lisette back with me to the States? No, even in the States we wouldn't be safe. Never safe until the perpetrator of these awful incidents was unmasked. I had to stay here. I had to help find our would-be murderer.

We drank our coffee, talking impersonally about politics in America, in which Dad took such an interest. Larry, here for another school year, was already considering his future in the States. He was determined to become involved in the politics in order to work for the betterment of life at home and bring to America some of the social benefits he'd seen in Europe.

Dad left us and went into the chateau. Larry and I became engrossed in watching a race between four sailboats down on the lake. We left the pool to walk to our favorite observation point for a better view.

"The second one from the right is going to make it," Larry stated triumphantly. He turned to me. "Watch and see—" But all at once his face stiffened with alarm. He stared hard at something behind me. "Down, Andrea!"

Bewildered, not yet reacting to what was happening, I felt myself thrown to the ground by Larry hovering over me. Shielding me. Simultaneously with our dropping to the ground, a shot rang out. Loud. Terrifyingly close.

"Larry," I whispered. "Who is it?"

"Stay down," he answered. "I'm going to find out!"

"Larry no!" I tugged at his arm as he clambered to his feet.

We heard the sound, in the greenery, of footsteps in retreat. Larry sprinted towards the bushes.

"I've got to try for a look!"

Larry disappeared. Shaking, I stumbled to my feet, my heart pounding, my eyes straining for a vew of Larry. He emerged from the greenery with a rifle in one hand. The handle was handkerchief-wrapped.

"He threw this away in his rush," Larry said grimly. "This may be our first real lead. Fingerprints. Come on, Andrea. Let's talk to your father."

Chapter Fourteen

"I turned to Andrea," Larry explained to Dad while the three of us sat in the library, "and I saw the muzzle of a rifle in the bushes. Aimed at Andrea."

"Larry pulled me down to the ground." I tried to keep my voice steady. "If he hadn't spied the rifle, hadn't pulled me down to the ground that way, I would have been killed."

"Subconsciously I was aware of a shot," Dad confided with a look of pain. "I didn't pay any attention. You know the Swiss interest in target practice as a sport. It is not an unfamiliar sound in this area." Dad gazed with revulsion at the rifle that now lay across his desk. "I was irritated that someone was shooting so close to the chateau."

"And the gun is from your collection?" Larry asked respectfully. "You're certain of this?"

"Definitely. There is a nick on the stock that is unmistakable." Dad's face was stern. He rose to his feet, crossed to a case on the wall, pointed. "That is where the rifle belongs. Someone familiar with the chateau came into this room and removed it." For the first time Dad conceded that the would-be murderer was not a stranger. It had to be someone familiar with the chateau.

Larry leaned forward intently. Frowning.

"What about shells for the rifle? Who would have access to them?"

"I do not keep shells in the chateau." It was a gentle reprimand from Dad. "They are carefully stored in the garage." Where Henri had full access to them, I figured. "But anyone can buy shells for a .22," Dad pointed out. "This tells us nothing." He sighed. "I have asked repeatedly that the doors be kept shut at all times. Still someone—" He hesitated. Aware that the someone to whom he referred was not a stranger. "Someone came into the chateau and took the gun down from the case." But the family did no socializing with people in the village, except for Larry and Phillipe and the doctor who had come to attend Lisette the night of her tumble down the stairs.

"Someone known to the family," Larry said, almost with apology. "No stranger in the area would wander in, see the rifle, take it out of the case, and go out to shoot at Andrea on impulse. It was someone who knew the rifle was there. Who deliberately came into the room, removed it from the case, and went out to stalk Andrea."

"The fingerprints will tell us who it was, won't they?" I asked. "We'll have no doubts once the fingerprints are checked out." Death would no longer hang over my head.

"Provided we have clear prints," Dad stipulated. "And that we are able to compare them with prints on file—" He looked distressed.

My eyes swung to Larry's. Would Dad hesitate to check the prints against those of the residents of the chateau? We would all be compelled to submit to fingerprinting if this was to mean anything!

"Monsieur Laval, after what just happened, I don't think Andrea—and Lisette—should remain in the chateau another night. They should go into Geneva to stay at your apartment there." Larry's eyes were serious.

"Tonight?" Dad was taken aback by the suggestion.

"A psychotic killer, frenzied for success is on the loose. We don't know what he might try next." Larry gazed at me with apprehension. "We don't know when he might try again. It could be tonight."

Dad stared at the floor, battling inwardly.

"You are right, Larry. I will drive Andrea and Lisette into Geneva tonight. I will sleep over at the apartment since I must be in the city tomorrow, anyway. Tomorrow the investigators will come out here. But please, Andrea, Larry —say nothing about the shooting to the others. Nothing about going into Geneva. After dinner I will tell Maman and Lisette."

"Not a word," I promised quickly. But soon enough they would know that Lisette and I were going into the city.

"Now let us have coffee and put this out of our minds for a while," Dad said briskly. "Oh, the bell is not working. Henri will repair it tomorrow." He made a wry face. "Andrea, will you please ask Claudine if we might have coffee in the library?"

"Right away." I tried for a casual smile.

As I walked into the hall, I caught sight of Claudine's small, rotund figure moving with unaccustomed swiftness. She had been eavesdropping on the conversation in the library. Why?

I continued down the hall towards the kitchen. By the time I arrived, Claudine was banging pots around with unnecessary force. Intent, I suspected, on convincing me she had been here all the time I'd been in the library with Dad.

"My father would like to have coffee brought into the library," I said with stringent politeness. Knowing she detested hearing me refer to him as my father. "For three, please."

"Oui, Mademoiselle." She nodded stiffly.

With a start I was suddenly aware that Pat sat at the table in the corner of the kitchen, seemingly absorbed in a book while she sipped at one of her endless cups of coffee. So in a few moments, I thought drily, Pat, too, would know that somebody had taken a shot at me.

It might even have been Pat, I told myself ruthlessly. Perhaps I was too hasty in dismissing her as a suspect. It could have been anyone in the chateau.

I returned to the library. Dad was showing Larry his impressive stamp collection. I hadn't even known that Dad was a philatelist until this moment. There were so many things, I thought wistfully, that I didn't yet know about Dad. So many years that we must bridge!

Claudine arrived shortly with our coffee. Her face was cold, forbidding. I caught the glint of icy fury in her eyes as they rested briefly on Larry, and felt a sudden, desperate unease. Yes! Larry was right. Lisette and I must leave the chateau. Within hours. I wouldn't have objected to leaving right this moment.

147

It was astonishing, I thought, that with this chaotic alarm in me I could sit here with Dad and Larry and casually discuss the efforts of the World Health Organization.

"I am surprised, Larry, that you have not visited the Organization," Dad said with sly humor, "since you Americans foot so much of their bill."

"I have a friend who spent a whole year in London," Larry said, seemingly relaxed now, "without ever setting foot in Westminister Abbey. I considered that sacrilegious."

"Larry, stay for dinner," Dad said on impulse. I sensed he felt an odd security in having Larry here with us. And gratitude for what happened earlier. "Call Phillipe and ask him to come over, also. Claudine can always manage," he insisted expansively.

"Thank you, I wish I could stay." Larry was regretful. "But we have two fellows from school coming up for dinner tonight. They've just come back from three weeks in the Soviet Union. Phillipe and I are burning with curiosity about their reactions."

"Invite them over for after-dinner coffee," Dad urged, and then stopped short. "But we cannot do that, can we? After dinner I will be driving into Geneva with Andrea and Lisette."

Larry glanced at his watch.

"I must be getting on home now." He grinned. "We do last-minute housecleaning before guests arrive. Lest we scare them away."

"Walk Larry to the door," Dad said. "And be sure it is locked, Andrea." Did that really matter?

I walked with Larry to the door, listening to a brief, amusing story about his friends who had just returned from Russia. How I wished that he could have remained for dinner.

"I'll drive to Geneva tomorrow," Larry promised, aware that I was tense about the move into the city. "I'll call you before I leave. The three of us will go somewhere for lunch."

"Lovely." I tried to sound enthusiastic.

"Be careful, Andrea." With a swift glance up the stairs and down the hall, to be sure we were unobserved, Larry bent forward to kiss me. "Be careful," he exhorted again, tenderly. "I have great plans for us."

* * *

I dressed for dinner with my ears unnaturally geared to intercept every slight sound. I heard the muted record player in Lisette's room and Pat talking with Grandmère somewhere in the hall, about where she might find wallpaper to match the unsoiled walls of my room. Pat, who hated waste. Who hated me.

I debated about packing a suitcase for the stay in the apartment. No, pack later, after dinner. I'd need things only for three or four days, I told myself optimistically. Within that time the investigators must surely come up with answers. They must, with the rifle left so carelessly behind that way. Surely it was covered with fingerprints.

Dusk was settling in about the chateau. Across the lake the lights of France twinkled against the graying sky. When I went to the windows to draw the draperies, I spied the night watchman moving about the grounds. A waste of money, I thought. It would have been more practical to have him patrol the interior of the chateau.

When Lisette and I returned from the apartment, we'd come back to a chateau where we could walk without fear. It was all so senseless! Who in the chateau was so psychotic as to wish Lisette and me dead? Perhaps the same one who was responsible for the death of Michel and my stepmother. Phillipe felt so sure of that.

The record player was silent in Lisette's room. I glanced at the clock. Time to go downstairs to dinner.

At the head of the stairs, I paused, staring down upon Henri, who was about to mount the stairs. A coldness closed in about me. Was it Henri who wished me dead? Most logically, Henri—who hated women and hated Americans. But what is logical in murder?

"Mademoiselle," he said in a monotone, his eyes opaque. Concealing what? "Dinner is about to be served."

"Thank you, Henri."

Henri disappeared down the hall. I walked with self-conscious slowness down the stairs. Within three hours I would be out of the chateau. Why did I feel this heavy sense of impending disaster?

The others were at the dinner table. I sat down in my customary seat on Dad's left, across from Lisette and Pat.

149

Henri came in almost immediately with the sorrel soup.

Was it Pat behind that rifle this afternoon? Pat had been at the Independence Day concert on Tuesday, with full access to firecrackers; and that night someone tossed a deadly handful of firecrackers into my room. Pat could have made the phone call that set off the fire. Pat hated me for being close to Dad. *Was it Pat?*

Dinner was another of Claudine's masterpieces, yet I ate without relish. Barely tasting the soup, the chicken in wine sauce, the parsleyed potatoes, the peas, the green salad. Most of the table conversation was carried tonight by Grandmère and Pat. Inconsequential talk. Dad was unusually preoccupied, speaking only when directly addressed. Lisette, so sensitive to undercurrents, covertly inspected him from time to time with anxious, questioning eyes.

Over dessert Dad sprung his surprise. I pretended interest in my food. Lisette seemed stricken. Grandmère stared at Dad in indignation. Pat's eyes went opaque. She'd known. Because Claudine had told her? Or because she had fired the rifle?

Should I cross Claudine off my list? It could have been Claudine, who hated me from the moment I came into the chateau. Was she fearful I would supplant Lisette, whom she adored, in Dad's affection? How absurd!

"What do you mean, Armand? That you are taking Lisette and Andrea to the apartment? In the summer?"

"I mean," Dad said grimly, "that the chateau is no longer safe for my daughters." He took a deep breath. "This afternoon someone tried to shoot Andrea from the bushes at the left of the chateau."

Grandmère turned so white I was alarmed.

"Monsieur Laval," Pat protested, and quickly poured a glass of wine for Grandmère and held it to her lips.

"I am sorry." Dad was unhappy at his abruptness. "Maman, please forgive me. But in the light of this happening, I think it is urgent that I take them into Geneva."

"Armand, I think it is best you leave Lisette here," Grandmère said slowly. She was agitated but striving for calm. "Take Andrea to the apartment, if you wish. But I will keep Lisette in my room tonight. She will be all right." Her voice was stronger, more determined. "Nothing will happen to her, Armand."

"Maman, I must take them into Geneva," Dad said gently. "It is wisest. Please, leave this decision to me."

"I don't like it," Grandmère repeated. "I prefer to keep Lisette with me."

"When her life is in danger?" Dad chided, and involuntarily I glanced at Lisette sitting there listening so somberly. "Are you forgetting the intruder in her room? The business on the stairs?" Now he frowned in irritation. "But why do I talk this way in front of Lisette?" He turned reassuringly to her. "We will go to Geneva, the three of us, and in a few days we will return. There will be no more problems."

"Grandmère, I want to go to Geneva with Dad and Andrea," Lisette said beguilingly. "It'll be a holiday."

"I will go up and pack for her. Claudine will be busy with clearing away." Grandmère reined in her anger with an effort. Only her eyes showing her frustration at this decision.

"No," Lisette, objected with a piquant grin. "Let me pack for myself, Grandmère. I am old enough," she said with pride.

"Allow her to pack for herself, Maman," Dad coaxed. "Just enough for three or four days, Lisette. By then everything will be all right."

Would it, I wondered uneasily? Only if the fingerprints on that rifle would lead to an arrest. Everything depended upon those fingerprints!

"If you have finished with your dessert, you may go to your room and pack," Grandmère acquiesced. She seemed exhausted. Drained.

Lisette pushed back her chair, put her arms about Dad for a moment, and darted happily from the room.

My mind churned with unrelated bits of information which didn't quite fit into a complete picture. Phillipe was certain there was a link between the earlier tragedy and what was happening now. An inner radar told me he was right. Lisette and I were so close to escape. Don't let anything happen before we left the chateau tonight!

I forced myself to pretend an interest in the table conversation. Dad was glancing at his watch. He probably didn't want to start out too late, I guessed, though the evening traffic would be lighter the later we left.

"We will leave in about an hour," Dad announced as Henri served coffee. "Lisette can sleep late tomorrow." I saw the shock on Henri's face as he realized what was happening.

"Perhaps I'd better go up and start packing." I felt a surge of discomfort beneath Henri's sharp scrutiny of me. Henri didn't want me to leave the chateau. *Henri?*

"Have your coffee, Andrea," Dad insisted. "You do not require an hour to pack for three days."

I drank my coffee in swift gulps. Tension closed in over me. An hour and we would be out of the chateau. Let me go upstairs now, make sure Lisette was all right. Why had we allowed her to go up to her room alone, knowing what we knew?

I excused myself, hurried from the dining room, down the hall. Heidi waited for me at the head of the stairs. She thrust her huge head beneath my hand for the petting she adored.

"You've been climbing on beds again," I chastised her with mock sternness. "That's why Lisette put you out into the hall."

I walked to Lisette's door, Heidi at my side, and knocked lightly.

Lisette pulled the door wide.

"Is it time to leave already?" Her eyes swept guiltily to her open suitcase on the bed. It was empty.

"You have time, Lisette," I said soothingly. "Go ahead and pack now. I just stopped by to see if you needed any help."

"I was kind of dreaming," she said shyly. "I was telling Michel how we were going to Geneva. He thinks it will be fun."

"Pack now, darling," I coaxed. "So we'll be ready when Dad decides we should leave."

"I've never been on the auto-route at night. I think I'll like it." She flashed me a brilliant smile. "I'm glad Father decided we should go to the apartment."

It was an adventure to Lisette. She'd put out of her mind the reason for this trip, I realized with gratitude. I must make these few days in Geneva fun for her.

With Heidi slumped in the corridor outside my door, I

went into my room, pulled a suitcase from the closet. Not the one in which I'd stored my slashed dress. The days would be hot in Geneva, the evenings cool, I tabulated. I must pack accordingly.

I moved with compulsive haste. In ten minutes I was completely packed. Now I hesitated about going downstairs. We wouldn't be leaving for quite a while. Stay up here, near Lisette, even though Heidi was right outside in the hall. Stay here.

At loose ends, I crossed to the balcony and pulled aside a swathe of draperies so that I might gaze out. As always, there was beautiful stillness outdoors, which normally I would have relished. But tonight that stillness seemed to emphasize the danger which hovered over me, over Lisette.

I saw the unfamiliar car in front of Larry's house. Their guests were there for dinner. And then I stiffened to attention, I was startled to see Larry emerge from the house, striding towards the road. Where was he walking at this hour of the night?

I started at the light tap on the door.

"Yes?" I was tense, although Heidi would have barked at someone unfamiliar in the hall.

"Lisette," she said softly. "May I come in?"

"Of course," I answered with a rush of warmth.

Lisette opened the door, walked in, and closed it behind her. How lovely she looked in her red quilted robe with its huge patch pockets.

"Darling, hadn't you better dress?" I chided her gently. And then I froze, thrown into incredulity. My eyes were galvanized to the thing she was pulling from one pocket. "Lisette, what is that?" My voice trembling as I fought to block out what my mind knew.

"It's a cyanide gun," Lisette said softly with a winsome smile on her face. "I knew where Henri kept it hidden. I stole it. It's a souvenir from the days when he fought with the Free French in World War II. He keeps it to shoot small animals who ruin the gardens because Grandmère hates noise."

"Lisette, put it away." She meant nothing by pointing it at me that way, I tried to tell myself. She was a child, playing a silly game.

153

"No, Andrea." Lisette advanced slightly, the gun steady in her hand. "I'm going to kill you. And no one will ever know. They'll think you had a heart attack. Even the doctors will say so. Nobody will ever know I killed you!"

Chapter Fifteen

"What makes you so sure no one will ever know, Lisette?" My voice sounded strangely harsh in my ears. "How can you be sure?" Seconds away from death I realized that, somehow, I must stall.

"Henri told me! The spies used cyanide guns because everybody was sure the person died of a heart attack. The doctors can't tell the difference." Her eyes glowed with fanatic zeal. "They'll say, 'Poor Andrea, nobody ever knew she had a bad heart.' "

"But your fingerprints on the rifle, Lisette," I forced myself to talk. "They'll point to you. Dad's taking the rifle to the firm of private investigators. They'll find out it was you." Heidi was outside. How could I alert Heidi to trouble in here?

"I wore gloves." Lisette was triumphant. "Like on the American television programs. That's how I knew how to start the fire in your room. From television."

"Lisette, why? Why do you want me to die?"

"Michel told me to kill you." She was moving slowly closer to me. Determined not to miss this time.

"Michel told you nothing. Michel is dead," I flashed back at her.

"That's right." Her voice was all at once oddly hypnotic. "I killed Michel. I killed my mother. I put the red flag on the other boat, so they would take the one that would sink. When they pulled away from shore, I took the red flag and hid it so that everybody thought it had blown away in the

155

night. They wanted Father all to themselves. Like you. He loves me best! He always has. But you came here, and you confused him again! He didn't know anymore. You got in the way!"

"Lisette, put down that gun," I coaxed. "Let's talk about this. Your father loves you. He loves you very much."

"He will when you're dead. He'll be all mine again!"

Something in Lisette's voice—an eerie shrillness—must have reached Heidi on the other side of the door. She whimpered uneasily. Lisette was momentarily diverted.

I reached for a book on the table beside me and hurled it at Lisette with desperation. The book hit the arm that held the gun. She cried out in sharp reproach. I lunged forward.

"No!" she screamed. "No! You have to die! You have to die!"

Heidi barked vociferously in the hall as I tried to wrench the gun from Lisette. Lisette was battling with a fanatic fury, and with astonishing strength for a twelve-year-old.

The door sprang open. Larry charged inside, followed by Dad and Henri. Larry pulled the gun from her hands. Dad caught Lisette in his arms.

"Dad, she tried to kill me!" Lisette was sobbing hysterically. "She stole Henri's gun and brought me here to kill me!"

"Lisette, I love you." Dad cradled Lisette in his arms, his face white, his eyes anguished. "Didn't you know that? Didn't I show you? You are my child, Lisette. I love you. I love you."

Phillipe had been right. There had been a connection between the attempts on my life and the drowning of Michel and his mother.

* * *

Larry, Phillipe and I stood at the entrance to the chateau while the private ambulance drove away. Dad was going along with Lisette and the doctor to the sanitarium, where she would remain for treatment. Grandmère had been put under sedation and was now sleeping in her room. Pat was in the kitchen putting on coffee, with which we would greet the dawn.

"I was in the library talking with your father," Larry explained. "Henri came running in to tell us that the cyanide gun was missing. They were all concerned—Henri, Claudine, Pat, even your grandmother—about Lisette's mental state, which they kept from your father. There had been trouble constantly at the various schools Lisette attended. That was the reason for the constant changes," Larry pointed out. "Not that your grandmother was implacable. The schools asked that Lisette be removed. Your grandmother admits this, Andrea."

"Did they know about Michel and his mother?" I thought painfully of Dad, who rode with Lisette in the ambulance knowing she was responsible for the death of his wife and his son.

"None of them would allow themselves to believe this, to put it into words. But, yes," Phillipe insisted quietly. "Deep inside they knew. But they prayed it was something she would outgrow—and they protected her. They watched, and they were afraid. I suspected something was not right with Lisette. I told Larry. He was furious with me," Phillipe said with candor, and Larry nodded somberly.

"I couldn't believe she was psychotic," Larry admitted. "So lovely, so bright, so talented."

"And disturbed," Phillipe said. "Tonight while we sat around over coffee with our guests, Larry told me you were going into Geneva. *With Lisette.* During the day your father would be away. You would be alone with her. I told Larry he must stop this. I would stake my life on Lisette's being disturbed. On her being capable of murder. He hurried to the chateau to talk with your father. This was no time for delicacy. The truth had to be faced."

"But the intruder in her room," I stammered. "Her being shoved down the stairs—"

"That threw me off, briefly. But those things were engineered by Lisette to make her appear innocent," Phillipe pointed out. "She has a brilliant mind. She knew that to implicate herself was to divert suspicion. And she would have got away with it, if Henri had not discovered the gun was missing and become frightened. Like your grandmother, and Pat and Claudine, he lived in terror that Lisette would try to kill you. This new sister whose existence suddenly came to light."

"We heard Heidi whimpering as we started up the

157

stairs," Larry said. "I knew something was wrong. We stood out there and heard Lisette confess to the murders. But we were fearful of breaking in at the wrong moment, lest Lisette shoot you that instant. When we heard the scuffle, we knew it was our chance."

"Phillipe, will she ever be all right?" My eyes clung to his.

"She will need years of treatment," Phillipe said quietly, "but there is hope, Andrea. Yes, someday she may be normal. But always, she must live with the memory of the deaths she caused."

"It's cold out there this hour of the night," Pat called out briskly from the foyer. "Come into the library and have some coffee."

"You won't go back to New York the end of August?" Larry asked me as we walked, hand in hand, behind Phillipe.

"No," I promised. "I'll stay."